EMMA FROST MYS

NEEDLES AND PINS

WILLOW ROSE

BOOKS BY THE AUTHOR

HARRY HUNTER MYSTERY SERIES

- All The Good Girls
- Run Girl Run
- No Other Way
- Never Walk Alone

MARY MILLS MYSTERY SERIES

- What Hurts the Most
- You Can Run
- You Can't Hide
- Careful Little Eyes

EVA RAE THOMAS MYSTERY SERIES

- Don't Lie to me
- What you did
- Never Ever
- Say You Love me
- Let Me Go
- It's Not Over
- Not Dead Yet
- To Die For

EMMA FROST SERIES

- Itsy Bitsy Spider
- Miss Dolly had a Dolly

- Run, Run as Fast as You Can
- Cross Your Heart and Hope to Die
- Peek-a-Boo I See You
- Tweedledum and Tweedledee
- Easy as One, Two, Three
- There's No Place like Home
- Slenderman
- Where the Wild Roses Grow
- Waltzing Mathilda
- Drip Drop Dead
- Black Frost

JACK RYDER SERIES

- Hit the Road Jack
- Slip out the Back Jack
- The House that Jack Built
- Black Jack
- Girl Next Door
- Her Final Word
- Don't Tell

REBEKKA FRANCK SERIES

- One, Two...He is Coming for You
- Three, Four...Better Lock Your Door
- Five, Six...Grab your Crucifix
- Seven, Eight...Gonna Stay up Late
- Nine, Ten...Never Sleep Again
- Eleven, Twelve...Dig and Delve
- Thirteen, Fourteen...Little Boy Unseen
- Better Not Cry
- Ten Little Girls
- It Ends Here

———

MYSTERY/THRILLER/HORROR NOVELS

- In One Fell Swoop
- Umbrella Man
- Blackbird Fly
- To Hell in a Handbasket
- Edwina

———

HORROR SHORT-STORIES

- Mommy Dearest
- The Bird
- Better watch out
- Eenie, Meenie
- Rock-a-Bye Baby
- Nibble, Nibble, Crunch
- Humpty Dumpty
- Chain Letter

———

PARANORMAL SUSPENSE/ROMANCE NOVELS

- In Cold Blood
- The Surge
- Girl Divided

THE VAMPIRES OF SHADOW HILLS SERIES

- Flesh and Blood

- Blood and Fire
- Fire and Beauty
- Beauty and Beasts
- Beasts and Magic
- Magic and Witchcraft
- Witchcraft and War
- War and Order
- Order and Chaos
- Chaos and Courage

THE AFTERLIFE SERIES

- Beyond
- Serenity
- Endurance
- Courageous

THE WOLFBOY CHRONICLES

- A Gypsy Song
- I am WOLF

DAUGHTERS OF THE JAGUAR

- Savage
- Broken

Someone's always watching me
Someone's always there
When I'm sleeping he just waits,
and he stares

Someone's always standing in
the darkest corner of my room
He's tall and wears a suit in black,
dressed like the perfect groom

Where are you going?
Why won't you stay?
They might be scared of you,
but I just want to play

He has no face
He hides with the trees
He loves little children when they beg and scream...
Please!

SLENDY'S LULLABY BY LILYPICHU
HTTPS://WWW.YOUTUBE.COM/SLENDY'S
LULLABY

PROLOGUE
NOVEMBER 2014

Someone was watching him. Rasmus Krohn was happy to finally see his friend again. He turned his head and glared at the door to his bedroom, to make sure no one was awake in the house other than him. It was one in the morning. They should all be asleep.

Rasmus turned his head to face the screen again. With much eagerness, he let his fingers dance across the keyboard.

>Hi there. Where have you been?<

>Hello<

Rasmus thought he heard a sound, and turned to look at the door once again. He held his breath. Someone was in the hallway outside. He followed the steps as they walked across the carpet. It sounded like his father. The steps were heavy, not like his mother's that were usually light because she would be tiptoeing in order to not wake up the kids. Rasmus followed the sound of the steps and breathed in relief when they passed his door and continued towards the bathroom. There was a bump, then his father complaining and cursing. After that, the door was closed. Rasmus breathed again. He turned off the small lamp on his desk next to the computer. The light coming from under his door could reveal him.

He received a new message from his friend.

>Are you ready?<

Rasmus looked at the blinking message on the bottom of the screen. He heard his dad flush the toilet and the water start running. The old man cursed again, probably bumped his toe or his head, as usual, the drunk. Rasmus held his breath as his dad opened the door to the bathroom and entered the hallway again. He turned down the light on the screen to low and sat in darkness. Rasmus's dad walked across the carpet outside, then stopped. Rasmus's heart was pounding in his chest. He could sense his dad was right outside his door now.

Would he come in to check on him? Or to pull him out of bed and start beating on him like last time?

His parents had told Rasmus so many times not to use his computer at night. Especially on a school night. His dad would be furious if he found out.

The seconds that passed felt like years. Everything inside of him was screaming. If his father walked through that door and found him by the computer, it was all over. They would take the computer away, they had told him...even though Rasmus had saved up for it and paid for it on his own. It wasn't good for him, his mother said.

As if she has any idea what's good for me! She doesn't even know how to take care of herself, let alone her children.

Rasmus stared at the bed and wondered if he could make it over there if the door handle moved. He could sense his dad was out there still. He even believed he could smell the booze on his breath.

Just go to bed, you fucking drunk. Leave me alone. Leave all of us alone!

Rasmus's hands were shaking when he remembered what had happened the last time his father had come through that door at night. He still had the bruise on his back from the baseball bat.

Just go back to bed, you asshole! Find someone else to bother.

He felt the rage rising inside of him. The humiliation was the worst; the fact that he still couldn't fight back was painful. At the age of fifteen, Rasmus was still scrawny. No one took him seriously. No one regarded him as anyone. But soon, they would. He was going to make sure of that.

The steps moved on across the carpet and Rasmus breathed again. He heard the door to his parents' bedroom shut and everything go quiet again. He closed his eyes and leaned back in the chair for a few seconds before he turned up the light on the screen again. The expressionless white face of the tall and slender man stared back at him from behind the screen. He had written a new message.

>It's time<

1

NOVEMBER 2014

I had tiptoed around the cigar box for two weeks now. I was back in my house after the renovation which followed the fire, and sitting in my wonderful new kitchen with a coffee and a pastry, staring at the box on the table in front of me.

I hadn't opened it yet.

The construction workers gave it to me after we were allowed to move back in. One of the men handed it to me, telling me he had no idea what else to do with it.

"We found it when we fixed the roof. It fell out when we removed the old wood and replaced it with the new," he said.

The man in the yellow helmet followed his statement with a shrug, and I took the old dirty box out of his hands. It had been with me ever since. I had taken it in my purse with me everywhere, and taken it out now and then to look at it, but never opened it. Not yet, at least.

"Aren't you curious?" Morten had asked several times when he caught me staring at it. "Why don't you take a look?"

"I'm extremely curious," I answered.

Yet, I still hadn't dared to open it. It wasn't like me at all. What was I afraid of? I asked myself over and over. I didn't know. I kind of felt like the box didn't belong to me. Like I was intruding somehow on someone's personal life. Like I was supposed to find its original owners and give it back. But I had no idea who they were. I didn't even know if anyone would care enough about it to want it back. It wasn't an ordinary box. Anyone could tell it wasn't. It was dusty and dirty from being up there under the roof behind the wood. Someone had cared enough about it to hide it well for many years. Maybe it was of importance to that person. Maybe I was violating this person's need to keep whatever was in it hidden?

The thought only made me more curious.

I touched the front again and ran my hand across it. On the cover was a handwritten name in cursive.

Larsen

"Maybe it belonged to your grandmother?" Morten had asked, but it wasn't my family's name. It wasn't even my grandmother's maiden name. I didn't know any Larsen. It was a pretty common name here in Denmark, so it could be anyone.

I tapped my fingers on the kitchen table and sipped my coffee. I had decided that today would be the day when I finally opened the lid. My fingers marched across the top.

Just a little peek won't hurt anyone.

I tried telling myself that maybe by opening it I could figure out to whom it belonged and maybe get it back to the rightful owners. It just seemed so private. My fingers touched the front once again and stroked it gently, while I wondered what great things could be in there. I kind of enjoyed having my own little fantasy about what it would reveal, and some part of me was really afraid to be disappointed as well. Maybe that was why I hadn't opened it yet. Maybe I was simply afraid of ruining the illusion. I was afraid of finding cooking recipes or grocery lists or something boring. I wanted this to be special. That was also why I waited till the house was empty before I finally lifted the lid with the tips of my fingers. I held my breath as I finally pulled it off. I was about to close it again, thinking I had no right to be going through it, but curiosity won. After all, it could just be cooking recipes, and then no one would feel like I had invaded their private life. Maybe there were even some I could use?

Slowly, I looked inside. My heart was pounding in my chest as I pulled out a stack of letters, all neatly bound together with a ribbon. I put the letters on the table and took in a deep breath. Carefully, I untied the ribbon. All the letters were addressed to the same person, my grandmother. I opened one and started reading the contents. Two pages fully written from top to bottom in cursive using blue ink. A date was at the top.

March 22nd 1959.

I read the first sentence out loud to myself.

"Dearest sister. He is the most beautiful child in the world."

2

_____

MARCH 1959

*H*e is the most beautiful child in the world. I can't believe how lucky I am. Oh, sister. I wish you were here with me. You'd be as enchanted as I am.

Helle Larsen glanced at her baby, who was sleeping in the crib next to her desk at the nursery where she was writing her letter. She couldn't believe how good he had been. Only three weeks old, and already sleeping through the night. He was nothing like his brothers. They had kept her up all night for weeks until she finally let them cry through the night. It wasn't something she had enjoyed; as a matter of fact, it was the worst part about having a baby. To have to ignore them night after night till they finally gave up. If it had been Helle's choice, she would have kept going in to the nursery to take care of them to make sure they didn't feel left alone, but both the nurse and her mother had told her this was the way to do it. This was the way they had done it for years. It was best for her, they said. That way, she would get her rest, and the children would know who was in charge.

"After a few weeks, they'll figure it out," Helle's mother had said. "If you keep going in there every night, they'll keep crying. It's very simple. If you don't come, they give up."

So, now that Per already slept through the night, and had done so for almost a week, Helle hoped she wouldn't have to go through the same process as with the two others. Hopefully, it wouldn't be necessary.

"Helle!"

Her husband was calling from downstairs. Helle finished the letter, put it in an envelope and put her sister's name and address on it before she hurried out of the nursery, careful not to wake up her sleeping son. She rushed down the stairs. Her husband Claes was standing in the kitchen with his muddy boots planted on her newly washed floors.

"Where's my lunch?" he yelled.

"It's in the refrigerator, ready for you," she said, and ran to the refrigerator and pulled out a plate with four slices of rye bread with four different toppings. One with herring and onions, one with liver pate, one with mackerel, and one with cheese.

Claes growled and took the plate out of her hand.

"I didn't know when you were coming in," she argued, to excuse herself for his lunch not being on the table. Her husband was with the animals all day, or in the fields of their farm, and only had a short time to eat. And it was never at the same time that he decided it was time to eat. He was always busy and always grumpy.

Helle never took much notice of his moods, especially not since she had the baby. Nothing in the world could make her unhappy these days. Not even Claes' growling or complaining.

"What, no egg today? What about pork roast? You know how much I love the pork roast."

"I thought you'd like something else today, so I gave you mackerel instead," she said, listening carefully in case Per woke up. She missed him so much when he was sleeping. "The doctor told me fish is so good for you."

Claes grumbled while he ate. It had been a long time since Helle had lost any interest she might have had in the man, and now she felt less than ever for him. But, he provided well for the family, and with that she was content. He worked hard on their farm and gave her a life where she could take care of her three sons without having to work much, other than help him out here and there with the feeding of the pigs and such. Helle poured Claes a schnapps to go with the herring. It stopped the growling.

"Where are Ulrik and Peter?" she asked. The two older boys always helped out around the farm on weekends when they didn't have school. Helle had prepared lunches for them as well, and put them in the fridge.

The mention of their names made the growling come back. Claes chewed loudly, smacking his mouth, sounding much like the pigs in the pen. He'd even started to look like one over the years, she thought to herself with a grin.

"I told them to run their bikes down to old Hansen and ask him if he needs any help."

Claes growled and ate some more. Helle regained some of her affection for the man and remembered why she had liked him when they got married. He was very generous beneath that grumpy exterior. He could be so considerate. Old Hansen had recently slipped and hurt his hip, and he had no sons to take over the farm after him, or to take care of him when he needed it. Claes desperately needed the boys' help around his own farm, so it was a huge gesture on his part.

"That was nice of you," she said. "They'll eat when they get back."

Just as she had said those last words, she heard Per cry from upstairs and rushed up to get him, while smiling at the prospect of being able to spend time with her baby again.

3

NOVEMBER 2014

Ulrik Larsen was sitting on his couch waiting for the nurse to arrive. He glared at the picture next to the TV. Elsebeth was smiling back at him from behind the glass.

"What are you smiling at?" he growled.

She had left him a year ago and, ever since, life hadn't been much worth living. Still, he had to do it. He had to finish the race. Even if it meant becoming as helpless as a baby again. Life had a way with irony, hadn't it? Here he was at the end of his life, and he couldn't even go to the bathroom alone. They had given him a diaper. He peed through a hole in the side into a small plastic bag that they changed every morning and evening.

At least they hadn't put him in a home yet. He was grateful for that. It was part of a new politic, his daughter had explained to him. They wanted the elderly to stay in their homes for as long as possible, so instead they would send a nurse twice a day. In the morning to get him out of bed, remove the diaper and change the bag, then once again in the evening to put him to bed. During the day, he didn't do much except sleep. The city sent someone else over with food on a small tray...enough for three meals during the day. Tasteless colorless food.

All he had to do was throw it in the oven or microwave and heat it up. They did everything to make his life as pleasant as possible, they said.

Ulrik would have preferred death.

The only fun he occasionally had was when he grabbed a nurse's behind with a loud laugh, or when he pretended to be senile and tried to kiss them while calling them his wife's name. After a little while, they caught on to him and started sending male nurses instead. That was the end of the fun.

Ulrik coughed and snarled. Where was that nurse? Usually, they arrived around nine p.m., but it was at least fifteen minutes past. They were never on time, but this was too much. Ulrik pulled himself up from the couch and walked across the floor of his old villa that he had shared for thirty years with Elsebeth before she decided to leave him. On the dining table that he never used anymore stood old withered bouquets of flowers and cards lined up telling him happy birthday. It was two months ago that his daughter had surprised him on his sixty-eighth birthday, along with her husband and children. Ulrik never liked surprises much, and he had hated this one in particular. It was his first without Elsebeth, and he didn't feel much like celebrating. When they had arrived in the doorway with balloons and flowers and food in their arms, he told them he wanted them to leave. But, as usual, his daughter didn't listen to her old man.

"Ah, don't be so dull," she had said, and stormed past him, starting to decorate the house while her good-for-nothing husband had started heating the food in the kitchen. Ulrik had tried to make them go away, and even tried growling at the grandchildren, but with no luck. Then, he had turned on the TV and turned up the sound, refusing to leave his favorite place on the couch for as long as the celebration lasted.

He grabbed his walker and walked with it towards the kitchen. He thought of the many nights Elsebeth had prepared coffee for them and always gave him a small butter cookie on the side. Sometimes—especially around Christmas—she would even give him a small piece of marzipan. Oh, how he missed those days. The small gestures of affection that he forgot to thank her for. He hadn't had a cookie or any marzipan since. He didn't even want to celebrate Christmas this year, much to his daughter and grandchildren's surprise.

"But, Dad, you have to come. We'll have fun. You don't have to buy any presents. We'd just like to be with you," his daughter Annie kept telling him.

But he wasn't going. He was waiting for death, and there was nothing to celebrate about that.

Holding on to his walker, Ulrik managed to get himself to the window to look outside to see if he could spot the nurse's car, but the street was empty. Maybe they had forgotten about him? It had happened once before. They had made all kinds of excuses the next day and told him they were very busy and they had many elderly who needed their attention, so he had to cut them some slack. Ulrik had ended up sitting in his own feces all night long on the couch, unable to do anything about it. He hadn't thought it called for him to cut them any slack. But what could he do? Like a baby depended on his mother, so did he depend on their help.

In anger, Ulrik turned to walk back to the couch, fearing that was where he would end up spending the night, since he couldn't get into his bed on his own. As he made the turn, he stared into a white expressionless face.

Finally, death had come for him, he thought, but much to his regret, he didn't feel the satisfaction he had thought he would feel in this moment. It wasn't a feeling of relief that had taken ahold of him. In the seconds the knife sunk into his chest, he was grabbed by a strange fear, and his entire body protested at having to leave now. He let go of the walker and tried to grab out at death standing in front of him. Desperately, he tried to scream, to call for help as he heard the nurse's car drive into the driveway. But he knew it was in vain. It was too late. His time had come. As the tall and slender faceless creature in the black suit in front of him pulled out the knife just to stab it into Ulrik's chest once again, he knew it was too late. Death had finally caught up with him, and it wasn't at all as pleasant as it was cracked up to be.

4

NOVEMBER 2014

I was completely swallowed up by the letters, and kept reading until my children came home from school. The construction workers were still working on my façade and had put a ladder up in front of my kitchen window. I heard Victor throw his bike, then his steps on the stairs and the front door opening. Victor ran to his seat at the kitchen table and sat down.

"Where is my food?"

I put the letters back in the box, and then sprang up. The memories of Helle Larsen's life lingering with me still as I buttered some toasted bread for him and topped it with strawberry jelly. I served the bread, then made some chocolate milk for him.

"So, how was your day?" I asked.

"You asked me that yesterday."

Of course. That was always his answer. I had to try something new. "Did you learn anything new?"

"I never learn anything new," he responded.

I buttered a piece of toasted bread for myself and thought about Helle Larsen preparing afternoon-tea for her family back in '59. Things were really different back then, but a lot remained the same.

They had eaten toasted bread with butter and marmalade back then as well.

The door opened again and Maya entered. I smiled. She looked tired. "Rough day, honey?"

She grumbled and threw her backpack on the floor. Things were becoming more and more normal with her lately. Since Dr. Sonnichsen had started working with her, she was gradually improving with every day that passed. She was becoming more and more herself. Even the grumbling and rolling of the eyes was back. I started to regret ever having missed it, but it was a healthy sign, and that made me happy.

"I hate school!" she said, as I placed her toast in front of her. She looked up. "I'm not gonna eat that. How old do you think I am?"

I shrugged and sat down. I took a bite of my own toast. It tasted wonderful.

"It's filled with carbs," she said.

I chuckled. Yup, she was definitely back to normal again. Well, almost. She still had some huge gaps in her memory that I sincerely hoped she would regain. It was frustrating for her from time to time, especially when talking to friends, that she couldn't remember things they had done together. Her short-term memory worked perfectly, but her childhood, and especially the time up until the car-accident, she had almost no recollection of. She remembered her father losing control and hitting both Maya and his new wife. That was why she had run away. But other than that, she remembered nothing. I was unsure if she was ever going to. Dr. Sonnichsen had told me she might block it all out because of how traumatic it had been for her, and that it would come back to her if she ever let it, if she felt like she was ready to deal with it. For some, it never came back.

"You want me to make something else for you?" I asked.

"You have jelly on your teeth, Mom," she snarled. "It looks gross."

I smiled widely to show it to her better. She made a grimace and I laughed.

"That is so disgusting, Mom." Maya got up. "I'm going to my room."

"You're not eating?" I asked, finally licking the jelly off of my teeth. I was worried about Maya. She was hardly eating lately. "I can make you something else. Maybe some yogurt? Or a banana?"

She shook her head. "I'm good. Dr. Sonnichsen is going to be here in an hour, and I want to go on the computer before she gets here."

"So now the computer is more important than eating?" I asked. "What about spending time with your family?"

She scoffed. "What family? You're always with Morten. And my dad? Well, I don't even really know who he is, do I?"

"You have a father. Michael is your father," I argued, but wasn't convincing.

"We both know that isn't true," she said. "I don't even want to see him anymore. There's no reason to."

I couldn't argue against that. He wasn't her real father, and after what he had done to her, I wasn't going to let him into her life anytime soon anyway. Michael was desperately trying to get custody of Victor, even though he hadn't shown much interest in the boy over the last several years. So far, he didn't have much of a case, and I wasn't giving him one.

"Well, you need to eat at some point. You didn't have any breakfast either. Did you eat anything at school at all?"

Maya didn't answer. She grabbed her backpack and stormed out of the kitchen. Seconds later, I heard her slam the door to her room. She had been on the computer a lot lately, and I hadn't decided whether I thought it was a good idea or not. She seemed to be shutting out the world and everyone who loved her.

5

NOVEMBER 2014

Her bags were heavy. At the age of sixty-nine, Jonna Frederiksen wasn't as strong as she used to be. Carrying her grocery bags to her bike alone was getting more and more difficult, but she did it. Jonna refused to let her age define her. She was still strong; she rode her bike downtown every day, where she went shopping or ran errands. She cooked for herself, and never had any outside help. She was in great health for her age, Dr. Williamsen told her every year at her yearly check-up. Her eyes weren't what they used to be, so she could no longer drive her car, but that didn't bother Jonna much. She loved riding her bike across Nordby and greeting her neighbors, as well as the tourists she met on her way. She loved the strong sea breeze and the smell of seaweed.

She walked out of the sliding doors of SuperBrugsen and put her grocery bag and purse in the basket on her bike. Then, she counted on her fingers. Six items. She knew she had to get six items today.

"Milk, coffee, a Swiss roll, lamb chops, green beans and potatoes." Yes she had everything she needed. Jonna never made a list before going to the store. That way, she was forced to remember what she needed. She just counted the items she needed to get, then forced herself to remember what they were. It was her way of keeping dementia as far away as possible. That was the only thing Jonna ever feared...losing her mind and not be able to remember her loved ones. Her mother had suffered from dementia for years before she died. Jonna was determined to never let it happen to her.

Jonna found the key and unlocked the chain on her bike. As she was about to pull the bike out onto the sidewalk, a car suddenly drove past her, then stopped and backed up. A woman jumped out of the car and approached Jonna. She was tall and had broad shoulders. Jonna hadn't seen her before in the area and believed her to be a tourist. The woman had a map in her hand and started speaking in bad Danish.

"Please help me," she said. She put the map on the front of the car and asked Jonna to come closer and look at the map with her. "Please. Could you help? I need to find Mindevej."

Jonna scoffed. She looked skeptically at the woman. "There is no such thing as Mindevej here on the island," she said.

"Yes, yes," the woman kept saying. "Mindevej."

Jonna shook her head. She didn't move any closer to the woman, even though she kept asking her to come and look at the map.

I wasn't born yesterday, you know.

She glared at her purse in the basket, just as a man stepped out of the car as well. He spoke to her in a language she didn't understand. It sounded Eastern European. Jonna held on to her bike and started walking. "I'm sorry. I don't understand what you're saying. I have to go..."

"Stop!" the man said.

There wasn't a soul on the street outside the store. No one to help if they tried anything. Maren, the cashier inside the store wouldn't be able to hear her if she screamed. A car drove by, but they didn't notice anything. Jonna didn't know them either. Probably tourists. Why people came to Fanoe Island at this time of year, she didn't understand. It was cold and clammy, and only someone who grew up here would fully be able to appreciate the cold wind biting the cheeks and the moist foggy air that came in from the North Sea. Still, she was always happy to see tourists. There hadn't been many this year.

"What do you want?" Jonna asked harshly. She had heard about these Eastern Europeans coming to Denmark since the borders were opened and robbing elderly people. She had heard the stories and read about them in the papers. But never had she heard about them coming to her wonderful small island.

The woman tried to talk and distract Jonna, while the man tried to put his hand inside her basket and grab her wallet. Jonna saw it and grabbed his arm holding the purse. She looked into his eyes while twisting his arm. Then, she grabbed his ear with the other hand and twisted it. She hadn't raised four grubby boys without learning a trick or two. The big man squirmed and crouched.

"Ouch!"

"So, you're trying to steal from an old woman, huh? Is that how your mother raised you? I bet she's very disappointed in you, young man. I know I would be. No son of mine would get away with attacking a skinny old woman on the street like this. How pathetic. Pick someone your own size next time. Now, let go of the purse, young man."

He did as he was told with a small whimper.

"Now I suggest you and that tramp of a woman you're holding on to, I suggest you get the hell out of here before I get really angry."

Jonna let go of the man and watched him sprint for the car. Seconds later, he and the woman and the gray station wagon were out of sight. Left on the sidewalk was Jonna with her purse in her hand and heart pounding heavily in her chest. She held on to her bike for a little while, catching her breath. Then she snorted and got on her bike. She started riding it down the street, shaking her head, and waving at her neighbors as she passed them.

"Attacking a poor old woman in broad daylight, is that what we've come to? Is that where this world is going? Someone ought to do something."

6

NOVEMBER 2014

"There was an old lady who was assaulted outside of SuperBrugsen today."

Morten and I were sitting in front of the TV watching a program about border patrol in Australia. Morten had come directly from work and told me he was staying the night. When I asked him how Jytte felt about that, he simply said *she'll live*. Morten had certainly changed in his approach to his daughter, and I was glad to feel she was no longer running the show. She was less fond of me than ever. To be frank, she hated my guts, but at least I had my boyfriend back. I had thought about asking him to move in, but knew we had to wait till Jytte moved away from home in a year or so. I still felt like he was spoiling her too much by giving her everything she pointed at, but had decided it was none of my business. Lord knows, my daughter wasn't the best behaved among girls either. They were just being teenagers. It was going to pass eventually, like everything else. Meanwhile, I was going to enjoy our life together, even if I couldn't take the relationship to the next level yet.

The officers on TV were searching a young backpacker for drugs.

Dogs were sniffing his belongings. They were my favorite part of the show.

"I always wanted a dog," I said.

"Were you even listening?" Morten asked.

I was leaning against his shoulder on the couch. "Yes, sorry. I heard you. A woman was assaulted?"

"A sixty-nine year old woman. She described the attackers as Eastern European. They tried to steal her purse. They've had a lot of trouble with these types on the mainland the last couple of years. I hope this doesn't mean they've found their way here. I really don't want this kind of stuff on our little island. It's bad for tourism and really bad news for us. Especially now that they're talking about cutting back on the police force."

"When will you know more about that?" I asked.

"Next week, I think. I tell you, I'm not looking forward to it."

"Is the woman alright?" I asked, as the dog found something and sniffed it closely. The officer pulled the dog back and started searching the pocket of the backpack. I loved the dogs. They always found something.

"Yes, apparently she chased them off."

"Who was it? Was she a tourist?"

"No, it was Jonna Frederiksen. She lives on the North side of Nordby. She was very shaken when I spoke to her, but not so badly she couldn't give me a very detailed description of the couple that assaulted her."

"I don't think I know her," I said.

"She's one of the real locals. You know, one of those that grew up here. Not moved here like you and me."

"I know. We'll never be real locals, not even if we live here for the rest of our lives," I said, laughing. There really was a distinction between those that had lived on the island for generations and those that had moved here. Even if it was your parent's generation that had moved here, you still weren't considered a local. That was just the way it was.

"Look at that dog. Look how smart he is," I said. "And adorable."

"He is very cute. I used to have a German shepherd once."

"For work?" I asked. "Was he a police dog?"

"Yes. I lost him to cancer. I loved that dog."

"Did you ever consider getting another one?" I asked.

Morten shook his head. "No. When you buy a dog, you also buy yourself some sorrow. They don't live long. It was rough on Jytte as well when he died. I don't want to put her through that again. You should get one, though. It would be good for Victor."

My eyes left the screen, and I looked at Morten. "Why, I think you might be on to something there, Detective. I've read about how being close to animals, especially dogs, can help kids with autism. I am looking to do something a little more radical. I've been looking into doing more about his diet. There are a lot of studies out there about how a gluten-free and casein-free diet can help his symptoms. Maybe this would be even better. I think I'll take him to the shelter tomorrow. Wow, I can't believe I hadn't thought about this before. He loves animals. Thanks."

Morten chuckled. "You're welcome." He leaned over and grabbed a cookie. The officer on TV was now pulling out bags of cocaine from the guy's bag, and he was starting to make excuses. I felt happy. In this moment, everything was just perfect. Well, maybe not perfect, but good. Real good.

7

MARCH 1959

B eing the oldest, Ulrik Larsen was always a little concerned about awakening his father's wrath. It was easier for his two year younger brother Peter. Ulrik had, from a very early age, learned that he was responsible for both his and Peter's actions. That was just the way it was. So, if Peter got himself in trouble, Ulrik took the fall. It wasn't fair, but that's how life was, his father always said.

It seemed to Ulrik that life had been getting increasingly unfair ever since the baby had arrived. At thirteen, Ulrik was expected to be a grown-up. And act like one. So, when his father told him to go to old Hansen's house and ask if he need help, that's what Ulrik did. There was no room for complaining like Peter while they rode their bikes all the way across the dirt road and entered old Hansen's farm.

Old Mr. Hansen had fallen and broken his hip. That's all they had told Ulrik. And now, he couldn't work on his farm, so it was falling apart. He needed an extra pair of hands, Ulrik's father had said.

"Out here we take care of each other."

Ulrik loathed working with his hands. He knew it was his fate. He knew his father expected him to take over once he could no longer work. He was to run the farm. He had no choice.

Ulrik looked at his baby brother, who laughed and raced him to get there first. It was so unfair. Peter got to do whatever he wanted with his life. He could even go to college if he liked. Once he was done with high-school, Ulrik would come and work for his father. That was what was expected of him. It didn't matter that he hated working there. It didn't matter that the smell of pigs made him want to throw up, or that he loved to read books. Farmers didn't have time to read books. Farmers didn't go to college. Everything Ulrik was supposed to learn, his dad could teach him.

"I got here first!" Peter exclaimed, and made a skid mark in the gravel with his bike as he stopped. He threw Ulrik one of his bright and handsome smiles. It annoyed Ulrik how Peter had everything. Peter was going places. He would go see the world, visit museums, and read all the books he wanted, while surrounded by beautiful women all of his life. Meanwhile, Ulrik would be shoveling manure and smelling of pig. No wonder his dad was such a grumpy old man.

"Now, behave yourself," Ulrik said, as they parked their bikes, leaning them up against the wall of the white main building of the farm. A cold wind hit his face. Ulrik breathed in the breeze coming from the ocean not far away. He loved the sea breeze and dreamt of sailing away to exotic places.

Somewhere far far away from this island.

Ulrik didn't like Fanoe Island much. It was too desolate, he thought, and often dreamt of visiting big cities around the world. He dreamt of being surrounded by people, educated people who would discuss philosophy with him or art. He loved art. He wanted to visit museums and libraries all over the world. There was no culture out here in the countryside of the small island. Nothing but pigs and more pigs.

Ulrik was the first up the stairs, and his brother kept behind him as he knocked on the front door. "Let me do the talking."

Peter didn't argue. Neither of them were very happy to be at old Hansen's farm. The man had always scared them, especially when chasing them off his property shooting his rifle in the air when they were younger. They had spied on the old man and his wife, pretending to be secret spies shooting with peas in a sling at the wife, pretending to be shooting with guns. Those days were gone and old Hansen had only gotten older and angrier with age. Ulrik hadn't seen him in many years, not since his wife passed away. They had lost a child once, Ulrik's mother had told him. That's why they didn't like children on their property. The wife had never stopped crying about it. In the end, that's what killed her, Ulrik's mother had said. The sorrow killed her.

"What do you want?" The door was opened forcefully and a rifle was pointed at the two boys.

"Mr. Hansen? It's Ulrik. Ulrik and Peter Larsen. We're your neighbors?"

The old man chewed on tobacco and spat. "Ah, the troublemakers. What do you want?"

"Our dad sent us to ask if you needed any help around the farm. He heard about your accident." Ulrik looked down at the cane the old man was leaning against. He was holding the rifle clenched between his arm and chest. Only half of his face moved when he spoke. Ulrik's dad had told him that the man had a stroke. That's why he had fallen. It had numbed half of the man's face, and he looked crooked when he spoke. He seemed taken aback.

"Well...that's awfully nice of him, I guess. Well, you can start by feeding the dogs and the horse. I don't have many animals left, but those I have I can hardly take care of being like this. Then, if you could clean up in the barn over there. I can't get the car out and I can't bike downtown anymore with this hip. Your mother has been so nice as to bring me groceries whenever she went the last couple of days."

"Sure thing. Looks like we should take a look at the roof of your house as well," Ulrik said, when he spotted two buckets in the hallway behind the old man.

Mr. Hansen nodded with a deep sigh. "Yes. Yes, that would be nice of you. The storm in January took its toll on my old roof. Rains an awful lot at this time of year, huh?"

"I guess it does."

8

NOVEMBER 2014

L isa Rasmussen was preparing for war. Well, actually, it was just for the mayoral election that was coming up at the end of the month, but it felt just like she was going to war. Not just for her, but for her family as well.

She was making strategies, holding meetings, bribing the right people, and getting rid of those that weren't on her side. It was exhausting.

Lisa had her mind set on becoming Fanoe Island's next mayor, no matter the cost. This was her goal, this was what she had worked towards. And she had the public on her side. Every day, as she took her usual walk from her house in Nordby to city hall, she took her time to talk to anyone who wanted to. Even if it was just to exchange a few words, or to tell her how wonderful a job she had done cleaning up the town, or if it was to complain that the elderly weren't treated properly, that the food that was delivered by the city to their homes was bad. It didn't matter. Lisa took the time to listen to every problem and comment. She would grab their hands and shake them using both of hers, like she had seen presidents do on TV.

Now she was sitting in her house going through her strategies as her husband Christian entered the living room. He sat on the couch and put his feet up on the coffee table.

"Do you mind?" Lisa said. She looked at her papers. "I'm kind of in the middle of something."

"And I want to read the paper," he said with a grin. Ever since Lisa had gotten the idea that she wanted to be mayor, Christian had laughed at her. He didn't think she was ever going to be elected.

"The current mayor, Erling Bang, has been in his seat for many years. People love him. You don't stand a chance. People around here like things to stay the same. They don't like change."

Well, Lisa was just going to show him how wrong he was, wasn't she?

Christian sighed and took his feet down. "How long are we going to live like this?" he asked.

"What do you mean *live like this?*"

"You're never home. The house is a mess, look around. No one is at home to take care of the kids. I have to pick them up. You're never here, Lisa."

Lisa snorted. "Are you implying that I'm not a good mother?"

"No. You're a great mother. You just...well, you just haven't been around much lately. Amalie, Jacob, and Margrethe are all missing you. I miss you."

"You just miss me because I used to do all the work around the house, and now you have to help out," she said.

"Well, yes. That too. It's hard on me to have to do everything. This morning, I ran out of clean underwear."

Lisa snorted again. "Didn't I just cook you dinner?"

Christian nodded. "Yes, yes you did."

"Didn't you enjoy it?"

"The meat was very tasty, yes."

"So, what are you complaining about? I've even hired a cleaning lady to clean up after you. I'll wash your clothes tonight. What is it again you do that is so hard?" Lisa stared at her husband with contempt. She really couldn't see the problem.

"Honey. We miss you, that's all. I know you take care of everything, but...well, even when you're home, this is all we get. You're always on the phone or writing or occupied with all this stuff. The kids are always asking for you. Every time we pass one of those posters on the streetlights when driving, they ask when this election will be over so they'll get their mother back. What do you want me to tell them? I mean, I don't think you'll win, but have you even thought it through? What if you win? You'll be so busy, we'll never see you. What about Margrethe? You're missing out on everything with her. Today, the teachers at the preschool told me she was crying because she missed her mother."

Lisa looked at her husband. "She was crying?"

"Yes. Apparently she hurt herself playing on the playground outside. The teacher didn't know how it happened, but she has a bruise on her back."

Lisa felt how her hand started to shake. "They don't know how it happened? Weren't they keeping an eye on her? Who did you talk to?"

"It was Laiyla. You know, the one with the piercing and purple hair."

Lisa broke the pencil in her hand. Yes, she knew her very well. Never trusted her much. Lisa closed her eyes and counted to ten backwards to calm herself down. Then, she looked at her husband again and smiled. Lisa tilted her head. She liked that they missed her. It was a good feeling. She put her hand in Christian's.

"I promise I'll try and be more present from now on, okay? So, Laiyla huh? And you say she wasn't paying attention to what our daughter was up to? Tell me everything she said."

9

NOVEMBER 2014

I took Victor and Maya to the shelter the very next day. They were both very excited in the car on our way there. Well, Maya tried hard not to be, but I could tell by the look on her face that she really was. Victor was smiling and looking out the window at the houses passing by. I was excited as well. This was an excellent idea. Just seeing their happy faces would make it all worth it, I was sure.

Nordby seemed desolate, I thought, as we parked close to the main street. It was always like this in the fall. All summer, the island was overrun by tourists; there was so much life, and when they departed, it was all calm and strangely empty. At least it seemed to be. There was plenty of activity still going on. The mayoral election was coming up, and all the streetlights were covered in posters for candidates. I still hadn't decided who I was voting for. They were down to two candidates. The sitting mayor, Mayor Erling Bang had been mayor for longer than anyone could remember. It was the first time in fifteen years that someone had gone up against him, I had been told. Lisa Rasmussen was his opponent. I liked the idea of change, and of having a woman in charge. I just wasn't quite sure about Lisa. She seemed a little fishy. I stared at her poster as we passed one. She seemed to be trying too hard to look gentle and trustworthy, but all I could see were those mad eyes of hers. They gave me the chills. I had no idea why.

It was dark, and grey clouds hung over our heads, but it hadn't started raining yet as we crossed the square. I was cold, even in my winter jacket. I nodded to a couple of people as we passed them. I knew most people by now. At least I recognized their faces. Like most Danes, the inhabitants of Fanoe Island didn't like to say hello, but they would nod with tight lips if your eyes accidently met. For the most part, people tried to not look at each other. Especially at this time of year when the cold made you bend forward slightly while walking, and all you really wanted was to sit inside by the fireplace or the TV with a cup of hot chocolate between your hands.

We passed a few small shops, the local real-estate agency, the small gas station, then continued down Niels Engersvej where I stopped in front of a small house. I looked at my phone where I had the address on the screen.

"This should be it," I said.

We walked up the small path leading to the front of the house. It was a couple that ran the place from their own home, I had read online. They took in sick animals, or animals that no one wanted and found new families for them.

A red-haired woman opened the door.

"Hi, I'm Emma Frost. I called about looking at a dog?"

The woman smiled. She seemed nice. She reached out her hand and grabbed mine. "I know who you are. Yes, come on inside. So, these two are the lucky children, huh?"

"Yes, well. We're just looking for now."

The red-haired woman laughed. "That's what they all say. But once you set your eyes on one, you can't let go. Come on in. I'm Camilla, by the way. My husband Poul is in the living room with the dogs. He brought them all into the playpen so you could take a look."

We walked inside, and the pungent odor of wet dogs and animal food hit my face. I could hear barking in the distance, and the sound of animals moving in cages.

"We have birds and cats as well, if there is any interest," Camilla said.

"I think we'll just look at the dogs for now," I said, and followed her into the living room. It was like a zoo in there. Birds jumping around in their cages, cats jumping around on the furniture, and dogs barking and biting each other inside the playpen. Victor and Maya rushed to the dogs and leaned on the fence. I spotted a small black dog that looked like it had some poodle in it. Poodles were smart dogs, I had read.

"That one is cute," I said and pointed. The small fluffy dog looked up and Camilla grabbed him and handed him to me.

"Oh, wow," I said, and held him close. He climbed up and licked my ear.

"He is very affectionate," Camilla said. "Loves children too. Fully potty-trained and up to date on his shots. He would be perfect. His name is Kenneth."

Maya came over and petted Kenneth on the head. "He's very cute," she said.

"And smart," Camilla said.

"I love that he is so small," Maya said.

"Small dogs are easy," Camilla said.

"I like him," Maya said.

"I like him too," I said, and petted him behind his ear. I handed him to Maya, so she could try and hold him. He climbed up and licked her face. Maya laughed heartily. It had been awhile since I had seen her this happy. "Oh, my God, Mom, he really likes me."

"I'm sure he does." I let Maya hold Kenneth and looked at the other dogs in the pen. None of them were as cute as Kenneth. No, this was the perfect dog for us.

"So, I take it you have fallen in love?" Camilla said with a wide smile.

Maya looked up at me. "I love him, Mom. I really do."

"Well, I do too," I said, while looking for Victor. I spotted him standing in front of a big cage at the other end of the living room.

"Can we have him, Mom?" Maya continued.

I stared at Victor. He put his hand inside the cage.

"What is that down there?" I asked. "In the big cage."

Camilla looked concerned. "Oh, my. That's Brutus." Camilla walked towards Victor. "You shouldn't put your hand in there," she said, but Victor didn't listen. Camilla looked at me. "He really shouldn't put his hand in there."

I walked to him. "Take your hand out, buddy."

I looked inside the cage. A huge gray dog stared back with eyes as white as snow. It looked like a pit bull. It had scars on its face and only half an ear. I gasped. It looked really creepy.

"I'm sorry," Camilla said. "He's not safe. Please take your hand out of the cage before he bites you. He's been badly mistreated. He's not well. I'm afraid we might have to put him down soon. You can't trust him. He bit my husband just yesterday, attacked him out of the blue. He can't be trusted; no one will want him."

"I want him," Victor said.

Uh-oh. I had a feeling he would say that.

"No, you don't," Camilla said. "He's dangerous, sweetheart. Please, get your hand out." Camilla grabbed Victor's arm. I didn't realize until it was too late. Victor let out a loud scream. It was ear-piercing.

Camilla let go of his arm and looked at me.

"I'm sorry," I said. "He doesn't like to be touched."

The dog growled and banged his head against the bars while staring at Camilla. It looked like it was ready to kill her. Victor still had his hand inside the cage, but it didn't touch him.

"Now, he's doing it again," she said with terror in her voice. "Occasionally, he bangs his head against the bars like he's trying to get out. I really don't like that dog. It's very rare, since I love most animals, but this one I simply don't know how to handle."

"But he lets Victor pet him," I said.

"That's...that's the first time he ever let anyone touch him," Camilla said. "I've never seen him quite like this before. It's very unusual; normally, he never lets anyone touch him...just looking into his eyes usually makes him angry."

Exactly like Victor.

I turned to look at Maya, who was playing with Kenneth, throwing a small rubber bone across the room and having him fetch it for her. She was laughing and kissing the small dog. His ears flapped when he ran.

This is not good.

"I want this one," Victor said, still staring inside the cage and petting the dog. It was now licking his hand and calming down from his touch.

I sighed deeply. There was only one solution to this, and I was certain I was going to regret it.

"We'll take them both."

10

NOVEMBER 2014

The numerologist had just gotten back from her session with Maya. She threw her bag on the chair, then walked to the kitchen and grabbed a packet of crackers. She was tired. Tired of having to pretend like she liked that family and that awful person Emma Frost. Today, she had been close to just grabbing a kitchen knife and stabbing the terrible woman with it. Just finishing it then and there. The idiot had taken both of the children to the shelter and had come back with not one, but TWO dogs. The house was a mess and a zoo. The dogs were running all over the place, barking at each other, and fighting. Well, it was mostly the small black one that had been feisty, while the big grey one had been quieter, and simply sat in a corner staring at the numerologist and Maya like it was carefully planning how to attack them and eat them afterwards. The numerologist didn't know which was worse...the small dog constantly barking or the big quiet one staring at her with hungry eyes. Emma Frost had told her that she couldn't say no to either of them, and she had preferred the small black one, but Victor really had his eye on the big one, so she had taken them both.

The numerologist had felt like yelling at her, telling her how

STUPID that was. How insane it was with two troubled children in the house. But she knew Emma Frost would never listen. She was simply too irresponsible.

The numerologist was happy to be home and put the laptop on her desk and opened it. Misty crawled across the table while the numerologist pulled out a cracker. Crumbs fell to the desk next to her laptop. Misty picked them up and ate them. The numerologist broke a cracker in two and handed one piece to the rat. It nibbled the cracker with great delight.

"There you go, sweetie."

The numerologist looked in her book and flipped a couple of pages. Things were going really well for her lately. Getting close to Emma Frost had been easy, and she had gathered a lot of material. Enough for her to take this to the next level. Yes, she had waited long enough. She wanted to move carefully, though. She wanted it all to happen in just the right way.

She flipped yet another page and drank from her water bottle. The stars were aligned just perfectly for her little plan to be fulfilled at this time. All predictions worked in her favor.

"See, Misty. All the books say the same thing," she mumbled, and stared into the computer screen.

It was true. 2014 was a special year. It was ruled by the number seven, since if you added all the numbers you got seven, making it a Universal Year.

The numerologist spoke while creating the web-page, sounding like she was trying to explain everything to her rat.

"The number seven is analytical and self-examining. It starts a turnaround as, even the mind, as cold as it is, recognizes that duality doesn't benefit anyone."

She looked at the pyramid she had drawn on a piece of paper. A pyramid of numbers with the year and seven in the center. There was no doubt about what this pyramid was telling her. The five in the upper right side spoke very clearly. The five represented a big change or shocking and unexpected event around November of 2014, and if she looked it up, the stars would tell her it was caused in large part by miscommunication. The numerologist knew exactly what this miscommunication would be.

She ate another cracker and tapped on the keyboard. A picture of Emma Frost was found online, one where she was smirking during a book signing, then a small video from a TV show she was on once, talking about her books, where she laughed out loud. She edited it so the video kept repeating her laughing, making her sound menacing. It was all placed on the page, and then accompanied by the text that the numerologist had carefully prepared.

"Yes, Misty. This is how it all starts. See, killing her for what she did is much too merciful, in my opinion. I want her to go down. I want her to hit the ground so hard she'll never get back up again. And then, we strike."

11

NOVEMBER 2014

Okay, so maybe I hadn't thought it through properly. Having one dog was a lot of work, but two dogs that were both new to the place was quite complicated, I soon realized. To my surprise, it wasn't the big one, Brutus, who caused me the most trouble. No, it was the small and gentle Kenneth that drove me nuts with all his barking and running around the house biting everything. He hadn't been in the house for more than ten minutes before he peed on the floor for the first time. In the living room. On the carpet. While I was cleaning it up, Maya came running and told me he had peed in the kitchen, and soon after, I stepped in a small puddle in the hallway as well. Frustrated and growling, I cleaned up again and again until I found one of my favorite shoes chewed into a thousand pieces in the bathroom.

"Maya!" I yelled.

She stuck her head inside the bathroom. "I think you should take him outside for a little bit. Take him out in the yard."

"But Victor is out there with Brutus right now," Maya said.

"They're dogs, for crying out loud. Can't they just play together?" I asked.

"I'm not sure the two of them should be playing together. Brutus could eat Kenneth in one bite without even chewing. And I think he wants to. That dog has been staring at Kenneth ever since we left that house like he really wants to taste him."

I exhaled. "Get a leash on him and take him for a walk down the street or on the beach. Just get him out of this house while I clean up after him."

"Okay," Maya said. She was about to leave, then stopped herself. "By the way, he pooped in the kitchen."

"Aaaargh! I thought he was supposed to be potty-trained!" I yelled, but Maya had left. I heard the front door slam, and suddenly the house was quiet for the first time since we got back from the shelter.

What have I done?

I finished cleaning up in the bathroom, then walked into the living room and looked at the damages. A pillow from the couch was shredded to pieces, Kenneth had left another puddle on the carpet, and tipped over my cup of coffee from this morning that I had left on the table.

I suddenly felt so incredibly tired. I sat down on the couch, thinking there was no way I was going to survive having these creatures in my house, when suddenly I heard a sound coming from the yard. I got up and walked to the window. Outside, between the trees, I spotted Victor and Brutus. What were they doing? Victor was sitting in front of Brutus, face to face, making it look like they were deep in conversation. I chuckled. Victor seemed so happy. I could hear him chatting with the dog. It was good for him to have something living to talk to for once. Usually, it was the trees and the rocks he spoke to, so this was, by far, an improvement, I had to admit. I didn't like the dog much still, especially not after Camilla had told me that they would take no responsibility if the dog were to hurt Victor or anyone else in the family. She really didn't recommend us taking the dog. She still wanted it to be put down.

Then, Victor stood up. He started walking around among the trees, and Brutus followed him. It looked like he was presenting

Brutus to each and every tree in the yard. The strange part was how Brutus seemed to understand every word Victor spoke. Nah, that couldn't be. Maybe it just looked that way. Probably it was just an illusion, but the two of them definitely had created a bond...and very fast indeed. That was a good sign. I turned away and started cleaning the puddle and the coffee stains, and just as I had managed to put the living room back to normal, the front door opened and Maya yelled, "We're back!"

I took in a deep breath and braced myself for yet another couple of hours of complete chaos, as Kenneth's barking drowned out every thought in my mind. Seconds later, he whirled through the living room and started biting the edge of the couch, while growling at it like it had tried to attack him first.

12

NOVEMBER 2014

Annie Holmgren was in a hurry, as usual, as she drove the car off of the ferry onto Fanoe Island. She was a journalist at newspaper *JydskeVestkysten*, her office situated in Esbjerg with a view of The Wadden Sea with Fanoe peeking up in the horizon. She was happy to be one of those who had escaped the island. Growing up there was more than enough. She had known all of her life that she wanted to leave as soon as she was old enough. She wanted to have a career and make it big. So, she had...going to journalism school in Aarhus, the second biggest city in the country, then off to the biggest city, Copenhagen, for an internship at one of the big national newspapers and later hired as a reporter there. Having a career had been easy for Annie, easier than for her husband. She had met Bjorn at the newspaper where he worked as a photographer; they had worked on many stories together, and even traveled together. But soon after their wedding, and while their first child was on its way, Bjorn had been fired. Cutbacks, they said. He had started his own freelance company, but hadn't had many assignments. Once their first child, Maria, came along, Bjorn had been a stay at home dad and Annie had cut her maternity leave in half so she could get back to her career. Bjorn had discovered that he liked it. He enjoyed being at home with their child. In fact, he had ended up taking care of all three children and the household while Annie focused on her career. Much to their surprise, they had both ended up liking their arrangement, him taking care of everything at home and her making the money. Yes, it was hard when they went to dinner parties and people asked him what he did for a living. It was tough on his ego. Especially in the eyes of his father-in-law. Annie's dad had never understood his choice. A man without a career, a man who didn't make money was hardly a man at all, he believed. And he never hesitated to tell Bjorn. It irritated Annie immensely, and over the years, she had visited her parents less and less. In the end, they only saw each other for Christmas.

When Annie's mother Elsebeth was diagnosed with cancer, every-thing had changed. Annie had realized her parents weren't going to be around forever, and she had quit her job at the newspaper and taken a job closer to the island at a smaller paper located in Esbjerg to be able to visit more often. She had helped out the best she could, since her father was old and not in the best health either. He was almost fifteen years older than her mother, and it was, therefore, the biggest surprise that she ended up dying before him. Annie had never had a close rela-tionship with her father; she didn't know much about him except that he was born on Fanoe Island, had grown up on a farm outside of Nordby with his brother Peter, and had lived on the island all of his life. Ever since her mother died, she had tried hard to make up for the fact that she hardly knew him, but somehow, it felt like it was too late. Her father had been away most of her childhood, since he traveled a lot for his job. He had started his own company. Annie didn't know much about it except they sold machines to farmers all over Europe. She guessed it was tractors and such. Her dad never talked much with her or shared anything in detail. He had, however, been very disap-pointed in the fact that she was a girl, since he believed only a boy could take over the business. But when Annie's mother hadn't been able to provide another child after Annie, and when Annie had refused to take over the business that had kept her father away from her all of her childhood, her dad had, in bitterness, realized his company would die with him.

Annie hadn't wanted to go see him today; it hadn't been her plan, but she felt like she had to. She had plenty to do today and had to be in Vejle to do an interview in a few hours, but since they had called from the city and told her that her dad hadn't answered the door for days, and that it had been locked when the nurses tried to get inside, she felt she had to go and check on him. It wasn't that unusual. They had been through it before when her dad had refused to let the nurses in for up to a week at a time. It had happened several times before, Annie had said to the nice woman who had called, but still something inside of her felt stirred and uneasy. She knew she needed to quiet the anxiety she felt inside of her. So, she had pushed the interview back a little and hurried to catch the ferry.

Annie rushed through Nordby and drove up the hill onto the street of her childhood. She felt a chill as she parked the car in the driveway and got out. She looked across the street to number seventeen where Martin had lived. The handsome Martin that she had had a crush on for several years in school. She had heard he sold refrigerators now downtown. Annie shook her head. So glad she didn't end up marrying the guy. So happy she was one of those that got away. Staying here would have made her lose her mind. No doubt about it.

"Dad?" she yelled, as she knocked on the door.

There was no reply. The sign saying Ulrik Larsen on the door had fallen down on one side. A lot was falling apart on the house lately.

"Dad? It's Annie! Open up!"

Still, no answer. Annie sighed and found her own key to the house, then opened the door. Newspapers and letters coming through the mail slot had formed a pile behind the door and made it hard to push open.

This is a bad sign, Annie thought to herself. If anything, her dad always made sure to get the mail. He was a decent man who opened his mail and read the paper every single day.

Had he gotten hurt somehow? Has he fallen somewhere and can't get up? Oh my, is he in trouble?

"Daaad?"

No answer. She tried again. A revolting odor hit her. What the hell was that? What could smell like that? Had the freezer stopped working? Had there been a blackout and the meat had started to rot? Had he forgotten to change the cat's litter box? Where was the old cat anyway?

"Dad, where are you?"

Annie kept walking through the hallway towards the living room where her dad was usually sitting on the couch when she arrived. The same couch he usually refused to leave. The couch he would sleep on if the nurses let him. But this time, it was empty.

"Dad? Basse?"

That's odd. He never leaves the couch unless he has to.

A nervous feeling spread inside of her. No, there had to be some explanation. Ulrik Larsen was a very strong man. He hadn't been sick in twenty years. Maybe he was simply still sleeping? It was, after all, still morning. But how would he have gotten into bed if the nurses hadn't been in to help him?

"Where are you, Dad? Are you in the bathroom?"

A fly landed on her forehead. Annie wiped it away. Another one buzzed her face. Soon three, then four.

Flies? At this time of year?

She had walked back into the hallway towards the bedroom when she heard a strange sound coming from the kitchen. A buzzing sound.

The sound of a thousand flies. Oh, my God!

Part of her was screaming to get out of there as soon as possible, but she felt like she was frozen. Like she was paralyzed. She was drawn towards it. She had to know. As she peeked inside the kitchen, holding her scarf up against her nose and mouth, her eyes started watering. Not because of the horrendous odor, but because of what she saw. Her own dad lying on the tile floor in a pool of blood. Flies were buzzing around him and his old cat, Basse, was gnawing on his face.

13

MARCH 1959

U lrik and Peter worked at old Hansen's farm all weekend, and the following Saturday their dad asked them to go down there again. Ulrik and Peter did as they were told without asking any questions. Old Hansen was happy to see them and immediately asked them to feed the horse and the dogs and clean up outside the main building.

"I'll take the horse, you feed the dogs," Ulrik said to his younger brother.

It was a nice spring day with clear skies and crisp air. Ulrik enjoyed being outside. He took the horse out in the paddock. The horse jumped and ran off while Ulrik closed the fence. Then he cleaned out the horse's stall and gave it fresh straw and hay. He poured food in the trough, and then returned to see if his brother needed help with the dogs. Peter was playing with the big labs in the farmyard. He had found a ball that he was throwing and the three labs ran to get it. Peter was laughing when they ran back to him and jumped on him. Then he grabbed the ball out of the mouth of one dog and threw it again. The three dogs all ran for it. Peter laughed. Ulrik smiled at the sight of his brother enjoying himself. There weren't many times either of them got to play or be childish anymore. Ulrik had watched his brother for a little while, when he realized he wasn't the only one watching him. On the stairs outside the house stood Mr. Hansen. He was leaning on his cane while staring at Peter. He was smiling too. There was something about the way he looked at Peter that made Ulrik feel uncomfortable.

Ulrik walked into the courtyard and yelled at his brother. "Enough fooling around. Come help me carry these big tires over here into the barn."

Peter left the dogs and ran to help his brother. They carried the tires inside the barn, and then walked back to clean up the pile of old garbage. All the while, Ulrik couldn't escape the feeling that old Hansen was observing them, monitoring their every move.

"What happened to Hansen's child?" Ulrik asked at the dinner table when they returned that night.

His parents exchanged a look. His dad dropped his fork onto the plate. "That's none of our business, son," he answered.

"He died when he was twelve, I heard," Ulrik continued, even though he knew it was a touchy subject.

His mother tightened her lips and shook her head. "We don't talk about it. Eat your potatoes."

"Why?" Ulrik said. "Why can't we talk about it?"

"It was a tragedy," his mother replied. "We don't talk about people's tragedies. It's also a bad omen to talk about the dead."

"What kind of tragedy?" Ulrik continued.

He could tell by the look on his father's face that he was pushing it now. His mother saw it as well. She looked at her husband before she answered.

"An accident. The boy fell or something; now, eat your potatoes."

"Fell how?" Peter had become curious as well now.

Their mother sighed, annoyed. "I don't know. We don't talk about it. It's none of our business."

"I heard he was trampled to death by the cows," Ulrik said. "That's why they got rid of all the cows afterwards."

"I heard he fell from the roof," Peter said. "That he was trying to run from the ghost that haunts that place. A ghost that kills children. It's true. He lives here on the island. He watches them for a long time, and then he lures them into the forest before he kills them. At least that's what some kids are saying."

Their mother looked perplexed, then cleared her throat. "Well, that's all very nice, but as far as we know, it was just an accident and it was very rough on the family. Let's not talk any more about this. Some things are best left in the past. Now, eat your dinner. You're going down there again tomorrow, your father said. I think you're doing a great thing helping the old man out. Now, eat."

14

NOVEMBER 2014

That night I had a nightmare. I dreamt of this strange figure hiding between the trees in my yard watching Victor. He was tall and had no face. He was wearing a suit and tie. His long slender arms were stretching out to grab Victor just as I woke up with a loud scream. I gasped for air, then screamed again. Right next to my bed sat Brutus in the light from the full moon outside my window. His white eyes were staring directly at me. My heart was pounding heavily as I crouched on the corner of my bed. I turned to look at the door. It was closed.

"How did you get in here?" I said.

The dog kept staring at me. He looked like he wanted to kill me. Those white eyes were creepy.

"What do you want?"

The dog didn't make a sound. That was almost the scariest part about him...that he was so quiet. It was like he was observing us, maybe planning his move on how to kill us all.

"Get out!" I said.

The dog didn't move. I pointed at the door. "Get out of here."

I got up and grabbed his collar. Brutus growled loudly and snapped at me. I gasped and let go, then jumped onto the bed.

"Victor!"

Victor came into my room, rubbing his eyes. "Brutus!" he said, and hugged the dog. The pit bull didn't make a sound.

"Would you get him out of here?" I said.

Victor looked the dog in the eyes. For a few seconds, they stood like that, and I could have sworn they were communicating somehow. It freaked me out.

"Just get the dog out of here, now!" I said.

Victor turned around and walked out of the door without a sound. The dog immediately followed. I threw myself on the bed as I exhaled, and then went back to sleep, thinking that dog was going to be the end of us all.

"I swear to God, the dog wants to kill me," I told Sophia when she came over for coffee later. The kids were off to school, and I was alone with the two beasts. I couldn't decide which one of them was worse. Kenneth was eating one of Maya's shoes, while Brutus was sitting in the corner staring at us, looking exactly like one of those porcelain dogs. It gave me the chills. I turned away and looked at Sophia instead. She laughed.

"It seems like you're in a little over your head here," she said.

"I told the kids that they need to take care of them on their own. I'll walk them once during the day, and let them into the yard before nighttime, but they have to walk them in the morning and in the afternoon. Those were the terms. I'm not taking care of that pit bull over there. He'll eat me in one bite."

"You know that's not going to last," Sophia said with a grin. "In a few days, you'll be stuck with walking and feeding and bathing the both of them."

I sipped my coffee and grabbed a bun that I had managed to bake this morning, even though the house had been in chaos, with Kenneth peeing on the floor and eating the furniture and Maya running after him screaming and yelling that she was in a hurry and that she needed to fix her hair. It was quite the circus.

"I'm taking them back, then," I said. "I can't take care of two dogs. There's no way. Especially not that quiet one over there. He freaks me out, I tell you."

I buttered my bun. Sophia grabbed one as well. Nothing like a second breakfast with your best friend. Sophia looked really well. I guessed it was the love between her and Jack. She had just been so happy lately. I was really thrilled for them. Really. Even though I had to admit that I might have been slightly, only slightly, jealous. I hadn't had that spark in my relationship with Morten for a long time. We were doing well, yes. Better than a few months ago, but still, I felt like something was missing. I couldn't put my finger on it. Maybe I was just bored. We needed to spice things up a little. I had thought about it for a long time and planned something special. Tonight, I was taking him to folk dancing class downtown. Yes, we were going to learn the local Fanoe-dance, and he had no idea.

My phone rang. It was Morten. He sounded agitated. "I'm sorry, sweetie. I won't be able to make it tonight."

"Aw!"

"I know. But something's come up. They found a body."

My eyes widened. "Who? What?"

"I'll tell you details later. I'm on my way down there."

15

NOVEMBER 2014

Lisa was walking with fast and determined steps across the square in the middle of Nordby. In one hand, she was holding an organic beet-carrot-apple smoothie that she had made herself this morning. She was wearing her long yellow coat and black gloves. In her other hand, she was holding her briefcase.

People passing her on the square nodded without smiling. Someone stopped with the intent of chatting, but she wasn't in the mood and kept walking, mumbling:

"Sorry, gotta run, important meeting."

The truth was, she had actually pushed back a meeting this morning because she had a very important errand to run. She sipped her smoothie while trying to keep her anger bottled up inside and not show it. She smiled and nodded at a couple passing her, while saying:

"Don't forget to vote on the eighteenth! It's time for a change. You deserve better!"

The couple nodded and waved. Lisa turned around and grumbled while sipping her smoothie. The numbers weren't on her side this morning. She was behind in the polls. Lisa had hired a campaign manager who had looked at the voters on the island and told her that her problem was that the people were afraid of change. They usually voted for the sitting mayor because they were afraid too many things would change.

"Freaking islanders," she mumbled. "Don't like change. Who doesn't like change?"

Lisa needed a cause, the campaign manager, Merethe, had told her. Something to distinguish her from the other candidate. The people didn't know her very well and that was her weakness. She wasn't a local; she had only been on the island a short while. Erling, they knew. He had grown up on the island and knew everyone. On top of it, Lisa was an independent candidate, and that frightened many voters. It was too different and made them feel insecure. She had to have something extra going for her to make up for the fact that she didn't have a political party to back her up. If they were to cast their personal votes for her, she needed to really stand out. She needed people to like her.

"Like me?" she grumbled, as she raced across the square and down a small street. "I'll make them like me if I have to. They don't know what's best for them. They're like freaking children."

She stopped in front of a house and looked at it. On the mailbox, it said Laiyla Ejlersen and Erik Ejlersen. So, she was married now, was she? Lisa finished her smoothie and crushed the cup between her hands. She found a trash can on one of the light poles right underneath her own poster. She smiled, satisfied. She had fought hard in the city council to get trash cans on every street. This was her doing. She was the one who could clean up this city and bring back the tourists. Tourism had been declining over the last two years. Many vacation houses were empty all summer and the restaurants were suffering for the second year in a row. Lisa had thought about making that her cause. To bring back the tourists. She had asked her campaign manager to figure out what was causing this decline.

Lisa walked up to the house and knocked on the door. A chubby young woman with purple hair and a nose ring opened the door. The nose ring looked like the ones bulls had. It was simply appalling.

Everything about her annoyed Lisa immediately. Why did people get chubby anyway? Didn't they have any self-control? She wanted to scold her and tell her to pull that stupid ring out and get a proper haircut and color in order to look normal.

"Yes? Hey, aren't you that..."

Lisa pushed her way inside the house. "Yes, yes, that's not why I'm here," she said, and walked into the living room.

"I am going to vote for you," Laiyla said, as she followed her. "You don't have to persuade me. I'm all in for change. It's about time we got a female mayor around here. Bring us into the twenty-first century, right?"

Lisa looked around, perplexed. She seemed to be home alone. "Yes, yes, mmm, well then, you're all set then, huh?"

"I guess so. Is there anything I can do for you?"

Lisa clenched her gloved fist. She hated having to lose a voter. It was really not what she needed. "So, tell me this, what was it that was so important that you didn't feel you needed to keep an eye on my daughter?"

Laiyla looked at her strangely. "What?"

Lisa waited for the light bulb.

"Oh, that!" Laiyla said. "You're Margrethe's mom. I completely forgot that. Well, I know it was unfortunate that she got hurt, but nothing really happened."

"Nothing happened?" Lisa said. "What do you mean nothing happened? She got HURT!"

Laiyla jumped when Lisa yelled the last word. Lisa closed her eyes and counted backwards from ten. It didn't help.

"I'm...I'm so sorry...but..." Laiyla said.

Lisa put her briefcase down. She clenched her fists briefly. "It's all you have to do. It's all any of you idiots have to do all day. Look after the kids to make sure they don't hurt themselves. It's ALL you have to freaking do! How HARD is it to do that?"

Laiyla backed up. "I...I..."

Lisa inhaled deeply to keep calm. So many amateurs, so many

incompetent people she had to deal with every single day. Didn't anyone take anything seriously anymore? Was it all just a joke to them?

Lisa tried to think of nice things to calm herself down. She thought of the ocean, she thought of the beach, but all she could picture was all the garbage people threw in the water or on the sand. Why were people so damn stupid? Was it that hard to clean up after yourself? Lisa tried to picture herself in a meadow picking flowers, but it didn't get her blood pressure down like the doctor had told her it would. She had recently been diagnosed with high blood pressure, and the doctor had told her to not get too agitated. It had worked for a while now, but not right now. All the anger she had bottled up inside from dealing with all these useless people surfaced in a matter of seconds.

"Are you alright?" Laiyla said.

Lisa looked at her and shook her head. "No. I'm afraid I'm not all right. I won't tolerate my child getting hurt on your watch, on anyone's watch. I'm afraid I have to set an example."

Laiyla looked confused. "What do you mean? Like, fire me? You can't do that."

Lisa laughed. "Oh no, you're right. I can't do that, but you know what? I can do something else."

Laiyla stepped further backwards. Lisa saw her look around to make sure she had a way of escape. But she didn't. Lisa was way too fast for her. She could run for hours on the treadmill at the fitness center without even getting out of breath. She was in excellent shape, unlike the woman in front of her. Lisa hardly ever touched carbs or gluten. They both knew she would win, even though Laiyla was younger. Her skin revealed a bad diet and her body no exercise.

Will people ever learn? So many sloppy individuals out there.

"Like what?"

Lisa smiled. Then she leaned over, grabbed the nose ring, and pulled it out. Laiyla screamed in pain and bent over.

"What the hell?!!"

Lisa slammed her fist into her face till she fell to the ground and no longer moved. Yes, those hours in the boxing ring at the fitness center had certainly paid off. Even though she still believed her behind was too big, Lisa felt in better shape than ever.

Lisa opened her briefcase and took out a big piece of plastic that she covered the floors with, then a saw, a knife, and plastic bags to put the pieces of meat in.

"I *was* going to make lasagna tonight," she said. "But now, I'm thinking a stew instead."

16

NOVEMBER 2014

"I'M SORRY I'M SO LATE."

Morten stood in my doorway looking like a lost puppy. I stared angrily at him. I was upset that he had cancelled on me on our very first night of folk dancing. It was supposed to be a surprise. We were supposed to go to the community center downtown where they had classes every Wednesday night. It was supposed to bring us closer together. My mom and dad had promised to baby and dog-sit. Now it was all ruined.

I didn't know what to say to him. "Well, I guess you had to be there," I said, and let him inside.

He leaned over and tried to kiss me. I gave him a reluctant kiss. He frowned. "Is that all I get?"

"Well I...I was looking forward to seeing you tonight, to spending time with you, and now it's almost bedtime."

Morten sighed. "You can't be mad at me for doing my job."

"I know. It's just...well, I had something planned and everything." I walked to the living room where Kenneth had gotten his teeth into my half-eaten box of chocolates on the coffee table. I pulled him away. Kenneth whined and paid me back by gnawing the sofa's leg. Brutus was sitting like a statue by the door leading to the yard. He had been sitting there since Victor went to bed.

"Does he ever move?" Morten whispered.

I chuckled and shrugged. "I don't think so. Not unless Victor tells him to. It's very strange. I tried to walk him earlier, but he refused to go with me. He snarled and snapped at me when I tried to put on the leash. So, I left him alone and hoped he could hold it until Vic came home. I think he did. He's the weirdest dog I have ever seen. But Victor likes him and they get along really well. I just hope he won't end up killing us all in our sleep. He looks mad enough to do it."

Morten threw himself on the couch. Kenneth barked at the sofa like he expected it to play with him.

"So, what had you planned for tonight?" Morten asked.

I grabbed a chocolate and put it in Morten's mouth. "Wouldn't you'd like to know, huh?"

"Well, yes. I'm curious as to what you could have planned that we haven't already done a million times."

The sentence felt like a blow. Was that how he felt? Was that how it had turned out? We had tried everything, and now all that was left was to wait to grow old together?

"Tell me about the murder," I said.

"Who said it was murder?" Morten said.

I shrugged secretively.

"Ah, you've been reading the case files, have you? You really should stop doing that, Emma. It's illegal."

"Only if you get caught." I smiled and grabbed another chocolate.

"But, if you've been in the files, you already know everything, don't you?" he asked, and signaled that he would like another choco-late. I planted one between his lips. He ate it with a grin.

"No, I don't," I said. "Someone hasn't finished his report on the crime scene yet. I want to know more. I might have an interest in the guy. I recognized the name from the letters I've been reading. Ulrik Larsen was the son of the lady whose letters the workers found. He's actually sort of family. His mother was my grandmother's sister."

"Ah. I see. Well, I'm not allowed to tell you anything unless you bribe me seriously."

I sat on his lap and gave him a kiss. When I let go, he looked like he was in pain, and I realized I was crushing his legs.

"Sorry," I said and moved away, feeling slightly self-conscious about my weight.

"That's okay, the kiss was great," he said cheerfully.

"Good enough for a bribe?"

"Will do for now. What do you want to know?"

"The scene. How was he killed?" I asked.

"We haven't gotten the autopsy yet, but he was stabbed and probably bled to death. The knife was still in his chest. The cats had eaten some of the body's face. It was nasty. Flies everywhere. Real ugly."

"I bet. So what kind of knife was it?" I asked.

"A hunting knife. I haven't gotten it confirmed by the lab yet, but I know a hunting knife when I see it. My dad was a hunter."

"One of those that needs a permit?" I asked, and debated whether to grab another piece of chocolate or not.

"Yes. It was definitely longer than the legal seven centimeters."

"So, you'll be able to pull the permit?" I asked.

"Exactly," Morten said. "We'll have this guy in no time." He leaned over and grabbed another piece of chocolate. I felt jealous that he was so skinny and could eat as many as he liked.

He smiled while he chewed.

"Got anymore coffee?"

17

NOVEMBER 2014

William Korsvig stared at the computer screen. He was waiting. Waiting for the slender man to appear inside of the house in *Minecraft* that he had built and where he usually showed himself to him when he teleported there. He never called himself anything other than that strange name. Slender Man. William had heard and read about him online. He knew he was everywhere, and that he was constantly watching William. He had no idea how, but the man was everywhere, including inside his game. But he only showed himself to William when he wanted to speak to him. He knew everything there was to know about Slender Man and wanted badly to please him. He would do anything he told him to. He could hardly believe he had been chosen. Soon, he would be part of something bigger. Soon, he would become one of his *proxies*.

Finally, he appeared. William smiled, feeling relieved. The skinny guy moved towards him inside the game. He was tall and slender like his name, and had long tentacle-like arms. He was wearing a suit and tie and had no face.

>Hi there< William wrote.

Slender Man answered.

>Hi. How are you?<

>I'm good.<

>Good. Do you know what to do?<

>Yes.<

>Excellent. You're ready. I'm proud of you, soldier. It's time.<

William broke out in a sweat. Slender Man disappeared from his house. William leaned back in his chair with his heart pounding hard in his chest. On his bed next to him lay his costume. He had bought it online using his stepdad's credit card. William got up from the chair and walked to it. He started undressing himself and putting on the costume, piece by piece. Black pants, white shirt, black tie. The white faceless mask, he put in his pocket for now. He would take that out later when he needed it.

William put on the black jacket that went with the costume, then grabbed the gas can and lighter, and put them inside his backpack. Then, he walked towards the door. Living in the basement of his mother's house, he had his own entrance, and could come and go as he wished. He liked the freedom it had given him to move down there, even though he knew it was mostly because his new stepdad didn't want him in the house and hardly ever let him upstairs, except to eat. His mother didn't care if he went out at night; she never knew what he was up to anymore, or if he even went to school or not. She didn't even know that he had dropped out of high school a couple of months ago and now spent most of his time in front of the computer or at the fitness center, where he had built up quite the body. His mother didn't know what he was up to and probably didn't care. William knew that, once he turned eighteen, he would be kicked out, but there were still two more years to go. William wasn't going to simply waste those away. He had a mission; he had found a purpose to his life now.

He opened the door and sneaked outside. He put the backpack on his back and grabbed his bike, then rode off. He biked across the small town in the light of the streetlamps. He swung around a corner and into a small street, then threw the bike in a bush and sneaked into a yard. He walked up to the house and looked inside the windows.

They hadn't pulled the curtains yet, and standing in darkness outside, William could see everything going on inside.

He watched an old lady sitting in a chair, knitting, then he watched the man half asleep next to her on the couch. The TV was on, but neither of them were watching it. From the outside, they looked like just an ordinary couple on an ordinary night of their life. But they weren't. William felt proud that he had gotten such an extraordinary assignment. He was proud to be chosen to fulfill this task. It was special. It had to be. The target was very special.

William put the backpack down, then opened it. He pulled out the gas can and started pouring the gas around the house. When he was done, he put on the faceless mask and walked to the front door. He kicked it in, then walked quietly and calmly into the living room. The woman sitting on the couch gasped and looked at him.

"Who are you? What are you doing here?" she said, and pulled her husband's arm. He grunted and woke up.

"What the hell?"

William tilted his head, then smiled behind the mask. He enjoyed watching the fear on their faces, just like Slender Man had told him he would. No, he didn't just like it. He loved it. He devoured it.

My God, this feels good. This is what it feels like to be alive.

"What do you want?" The man asked, and jumped up from the sofa. He was very agile for an old man. His cheeks were burning red with anger. He walked towards William.

"Is this some sort of prank?"

William reached out his long slender arms and slammed his clenched fist into the man's face. The woman screamed while the man fell backwards. William lifted the gas can and started pouring gasoline on the body of the old man.

"Stop!" the woman screamed. "What are you doing?"

The old man was staring at him, then screaming for help. William held him down, while making sure the gas soaked his clothes. He squirmed underneath William, but wasn't strong enough to get free. William secured him to the floor with duct tape, then stood above him before reaching into his pocket and pulling out the lighter.

"No! No! Don't!" The man screamed, panicking.

William turned his faceless mask towards the woman. While lifting the lighter into the air, he whispered:

"Run, little lady. Run for your life."

18

NOVEMBER 2014

"THERE'S A FFFFIRE ACROSS TOWN!"

Jack was standing in my doorway. He had knocked on the door in the middle of the night, waking everyone up, including the dogs. Kenneth was now running around behind me, barking loudly and biting everything he could find. I wasn't quite awake yet.

"Excuse me?"

"I thought Mmmorten might be at your house. I tried his cell, but he didn't answer. Is he here? He nnneeds to come with me. I got the call a minute ago. A house is on fire across town. I need him to come with me. I called the station and Allan, who was on duty tonight, is on his way down there, but we need as many men we can gather. It's a big fire, they say."

My eyes widened. Jack was the island's volunteer firefighter, since we didn't have a fire station. "He's still asleep. I'll go get him right away," I said, and stormed up the stairs. Jack came inside and closed the door. I heard Kenneth barking loudly at him. I rushed inside the bedroom and woke Morten up.

"There's a big fire. Jack is downstairs. They need your help. Allan is on his way too."

Morten jumped out of bed. I got dressed in a hurry as well. Morten looked at me. "What? I'm coming," I said. "You need all the help you can get."

He didn't even bother arguing. There was no time. I ran to Maya and woke her up and told her we were leaving and that I was leaving her in charge of the house and of Victor for a few hours. She growled and went back to sleep. I took that as a sign she had heard me, then ran downstairs and jumped into Jack's small fire truck that the county had provided him.

Soon, we were driving across town with blaring sirens. I could see the fire as we approached the house. It was big, all right. The flames were licking the night sky.

"I just hhhope we can stop it before it spreads to any of the surrounding houses," Jack yelled. I noticed he barely stuttered when he was agitated. "That would be a real tragedy. Lots of these houses have thatched roofs. The entire neighborhood will bbburn down in a matter of minutes."

Jack made a turn, and we drove onto a small street. It was narrow, but Jack managed to maneuver the truck through. We came closer and I saw people in their night robes in front of the house. They looked terrified. Probably neighbors afraid the fire would spread to their houses as well.

"It's the mayor's house!" Morten exclaimed, as we came closer. "It's Mayor Bang's house!"

Officer Allan arrived at the same time we did. We jumped out of the truck and approached the house. Outside stood a woman screaming and staring paralyzed at the fire in front of her. While Morten, Allan, and Jack pulled out the hose and attached it to the fire hydrant, I grabbed the woman and let her cry in my arms.

"Help him!" she yelled, her voice breaking. "He's in there! He's still in there! Help him. They gotta help him!"

"You mean someone is still in there?" I asked, horrified.

"Yes! My husband! Help him!"

I ran to Morten. "There's someone in there. There's someone in the house!"

Morten and Jack looked at each other. Jack shook his head. He was the only one wearing firefighter equipment, but still, he wasn't professionally trained.

"What do we do?" Morten asked.

Jack shook his head again. "I...I don't think there's much we can do. The house is almost burned to the ggground." He looked terrified at the thought of having to go in. I couldn't blame him. The roof was hanging loosely, and the loud cracking sounds told me it wouldn't be long before it crashed. I was right. Seconds later, it did. The entire roof collapsed on top of the house. The mayor's wife screamed. I ran to her and grabbed her in my arms.

Jack got the hose going and started spraying water on the remains of the house to put the fire out and prevent it from spreading. I held the woman in my arms and tried to comfort her, while I couldn't stop thinking about how the same thing had almost happened to me a few months ago. I shivered, thinking about what would have happened if we hadn't gotten out in time. If one of my children hadn't...I didn't want to finish the thought. It was too gruesome. I was just so relieved that the woman who had set my house on fire had been caught. I had a lot to thank Dr. Sonnichsen for.

The woman was sobbing and crying hard in my arms. I had no idea how to console her. She had lost everything in a matter of minutes. Her husband, her house, her entire life, all her memories, everything. There was nothing I could say or do. So, I didn't. I simply kept quiet and held her tight till she exhausted herself and could cry no more.

19

NOVEMBER 2014

"Do you have any idea how this could have happened?" Morten was looking at Mrs. Bang. She was sitting inside Jack's firefighter truck with a blanket over her shoulders, her feet sticking out the door. She shook her head. Her eyes were lost in desperation. The shock was visible on her face and in her eyes.

"I...I...there was a guy, there was someone...he...he broke into the house. He...he had a can of gasoline. He poured it over my husband, then lit the lighter...I thought I could run for help. He told me to run. *Run, little lady,* he said. So I did. I ran, but as soon as I was outside, running across the street to get ahold of our neighbors, there was an explosion, and when I turned to look, the house was on fire. It all went so fast. I can hardly believe it. I...I..."

Morten wrote on his notepad. "So, it was arson. Murder-arson, you say?"

Mrs. Bang nodded with a whimper.

"Did you get a good look at the man who entered your house?" he asked.

"Yes," Mrs. Bang cried again. I held her hand and put an arm around her shoulder.

"It's okay," I said. "Take your time."

"Can you describe him for me?" Morten asked.

Mrs. Bang tried hard to stop crying. I gave her a new Kleenex.

"Just tell me what he looked like. Was there anything particular that you noticed about him?"

"I...He...he didn't have a face."

"He didn't have a face?" Morten asked, puzzled.

"He was wearing a mask, but it was just white. All blank."

"Okay. So, he was masked," Morten repeated, while scribbling his notes. "Anything else?"

"He was tall. Tall and slender."

"A slender man," Morten said. "Got it. What else?"

"He was wearing a black suit and tie," she continued.

"A suit and tie?" I asked. "That sounds quite unusual for a killer."

Mrs. Bang shook her head. "This was no ordinary killer. I couldn't see his eyes, but I was certain he enjoyed it."

"Did he say anything?" Morten asked.

"Just *run, little lady. Run for your life.* That was right before...right before he...he lit the lighter."

"I found something!" Allan yelled.

Morten and I both looked outside. Allan was walking towards us with a bike in his hands.

"That could belong to anyone," Morten said.

"It was parked right at the entrance to the yard," Allan said.

"I've never seen that bike before," Mrs. Bang said.

"But still," Morten said. "It could be from some kid who stole it and threw it in the bushes afterwards. But, take it in for examination, maybe find out who it belongs to."

"I'm on it!" Allan yelled.

Morten returned to Mrs. Bang. She was shaking her head heavily and straightening out her skirt, while mumbling to herself. I wondered if she would ever again become a whole person after this. To be attacked in your own home like this was terrible. She would experience trauma for years afterwards.

"I'll take her to the hospital in Esbjerg," Morten said. "We can take the morning ferry to the mainland. It leaves in an hour and a half. I'll leave the rest of the questioning for later."

I stayed and helped clean up, but hours later, I decided to walk home. Jack had to stay at the site to make sure it was all under control. It took half an hour before I was finally at the doorstep to my house. I glanced at the façade when the sunlight peeked up from behind the horizon, behind the house. The light was gorgeous. I thought about this strange house and all its history and wondered about my grandmother's sister, Helle Larsen. Her son had been murdered, and now the mayor of the town had been as well. They weren't the same age; the mayor had recently turned fifty-five, I remembered from the local paper. Ulrik Larsen had been sixty-eight when he died. Could there be a connection between their deaths? Could it be a coincidence? After so many years of being mayor, he had probably made his share of enemies, but still. Something told me there was more to this story than simply coincidence.

I didn't get to finish the thought before the front door sprang open and Kenneth jumped out towards me, followed by Maya holding on to the leash.

20

MAY 1959

O ld Hansen's hip was doing better, and he didn't need as much help as earlier. Still, their father sent Ulrik and Peter down to help him out every Saturday for many weeks to come, and old Hansen was so pleased with their help. They fed the animals and fixed whatever needed to be fixed.

One afternoon, when Ulrik was done with feeding the horse and cleaning out the stalls, he started moving the bales of straw that seemed to take up too much space. He grabbed one after the other and moved them up against the wall, stacking them on top of each other to make more room. Then, he grabbed a broom and started sweeping the straw off the floor. That was when he came across something that made his blood freeze. Peter was right behind him and saw it too. A massive dried up bloodstain, right there on the cement floor inside the stable. It had, up until now, been covered by the straw.

"What do you think it is?" Peter asked.

Ulrik swallowed hard. He could hardly breathe. "It looks like blood."

"That's a lot of blood," Peter said.

"I know," Ulrik replied.

"Do you think this is where he died?" Peter asked. He sounded like he thought it was exciting. Ulrik felt nauseated. All those stories he had heard about what happened to Hansen's kid. Were they true after all?

Ulrik kept sweeping, trying to block out his brother. "I don't know," he said. "It's none of our business anyway."

"This place gives me the creeps," Peter said. "I feel like someone is constantly watching us."

Ulrik stopped sweeping. He had felt it too. It was like the old man was constantly watching their every move. He had hoped it would soon be over, that their dad would tell them they didn't have to go down there anymore, especially now that the old man was doing better, but it hadn't happened yet.

"Let's just hurry up and finish what we have to do," he said, and swept even more forcefully. Dust and straw whirled into the air. Peter sneezed.

"Gesuntheit," a voice said behind them.

Ulrik gasped and turned. The old man was standing right behind them. He was leaning on his cane, but not as heavily as he used to. He was walking with more ease now, but still needed the cane for support.

"Thank you," Peter said, and wiped his nose on his sleeve.

Usually, Ulrik would tell him to not do that, but not today. Today, he stared at the old man while a shiver ran down his back.

Old Hansen looked at the blood stain. "I bet you wonder what that came from, huh?"

Ulrik and Peter didn't dare to look down. Cautiously, Peter nodded. Ulrik didn't dare to even move.

The old man came closer. He touched the stain with the tip of his cane. "I didn't see it happen," he said.

"Was it your son?" Peter asked.

The old man stared at the stain. "Yes. Life never was the same after this. There were times I wondered if it was even worth living, you know?"

"What happened?" Peter asked.

Ulrik was petrified. Why did his brother keep asking these questions? Ulrik just wanted to get out of there.

"You don't know? I thought everyone around here knew," Hansen said. "Heard it through the grapevine, as they say."

Peter shook his head. "Nnno, sir. I don't think anyone knows."

Hansen shrugged. "Well, the stories they tell are probably better, then. They do tell stories about it, don't they?"

"Well, yes," Peter said.

"So, what did happen?" Ulrik finally asked.

The old man looked at him. There were all kinds of emotions in his eyes. Most of them were regrets.

"He killed himself. Shot himself with my rifle. Bang. Just like that, and everything was destroyed. There's your story. Not as exciting as you imagined, huh? Well, tragedies rarely are."

21

NOVEMBER 2014

I tried to get some rest once the kids had left for school, but with the dogs in the house, it was impossible. Kenneth kept growling and biting my comforter, pulling it off me. I put him in the hallway and shut the door. He went quiet for a long time. That made me seriously nervous. I walked into the hallway and saw that he had left a small present for me on the rug.

"Kenneth!"

I grabbed him by the collar and carried him into the yard. When I came back inside, I spotted Brutus sitting in the corner of the living room. He was staring directly at me with his strange white eyes. I paused. I didn't like the way he looked at me. I still felt like he was planning how to take over the house...or maybe even the entire world.

"Don't just sit there," I said to him.

He still didn't move. I sighed and let him be. He seemed to do whatever pleased him anyway. I couldn't understand how a big dog like that could be that quiet, when the small one created such turmoil wherever it went.

I walked to the kitchen and put on a pot of coffee, then went upstairs and removed the poop with a small bag before I picked up the rug. I put it in the washer in the basement, then returned to my coffeepot in the kitchen. The kids had eaten cereal and toasted bread for breakfast, but I had made dough the night before, and all I needed was to roll it out and make small buns to put in the oven, and they would be ready for afternoon tea. I had made them with raisins this time, trying to be a little healthier. I looked at myself in the mirror. My black sweatpants were tight on my thighs. I didn't feel too good about myself. I decided to cut back on the sweets and maybe start running on the beach. The thought made me tired. Why did it have to be like that? Maybe there was some machine I could buy? I certainly wasn't going to try any of those diet pills that people used. I wasn't that desperate. One of my childhood friends had started Herbalife at the age of eighteen and put on so much weight within the first year, I could hardly recognize her. Still, she swore it was good for her to keep using the product, and even tried to sell it to her friends, including me.

I walked back to the kitchen and poured myself a big cup of coffee. I really needed it. I pulled my laptop closer and turned it on. I wondered about the fire and the mayor and if there was any news on the tall slender man in the black suit. I couldn't help thinking that I had heard about a similar figure before, but I couldn't remember where. I hacked into the police case files and found that Morten hadn't written his report on the fire last night yet. I wondered if he was even back from Esbjerg, and called him. He had just gotten back. It had been hard, he said. Mrs. Bang had asked him to stay while she talked to the doctors. She was scared of being alone. She had always been with Erling. He had taken care of everything. Now, she had no one. So, Morten had stayed a little while, till the doctors gave her something to make her fall asleep. Then, he had finally left and taken the ferry back. Morten and I talked for a little while, but he was busy and about to write his report, he told me. The town was in a state of shock at the loss of its mayor right before the election.

"Okay. I'll let you get back to work. But tell me first if you found anything new. What about the knife used to kill Ulrik Larsen? You said you might be able to track it. Have you found out who owns it yet?"

"As a matter of fact, I just received the serial number," he said. "I'll pull it out of the system as soon as possible. First, I need to go to the bathroom, then I'm getting a cup of coffee, and I'll be right on it. Talk to you later."

He hung up and I put the phone down. I sipped my coffee and was wondering whether there was any chocolate in the cabinet, when the front door opened.

"Hello?"

It was Sophia. She rushed into the kitchen.

"Easy there," I said with a grin. "There's coffee enough for the both of us."

"Have you seen it?" Sophia looked at the computer on my table. I hadn't had the time to open any programs yet.

"Seen what? If you're talking about the fire last night that killed the mayor, then yes. I saw it all. Coffee?"

"Yes, please," Sophia said, and sat down. I could hear Kenneth barking on the back porch and scraping the door, wanting to get inside.

"And you better get a refill as well. You're going to need it," Sophia continued.

I frowned. "That sounds serious. What's up?"

Sophia grabbed my computer and opened the Internet. I served us both some coffee, then sat down next to her.

"What's up with him?" Sophia asked, and turned her head.

I looked in the same direction and spotted Brutus sitting in the corner of the room, staring at us.

"Where the heck did he come from?" I asked. The door to the kitchen was still closed. How did he get in? "Brutus! Stop staring at us. I swear, that dog freaks me out," I said, and looked at Sophia.

"Not as much as this will," she said, and turned the screen so I could see.

It was a Facebook page. It had my picture as the cover and as the profile picture. The pictures weren't very flattering. The name of the page was:

I HATE EMMA FROST.

What the heck?

Baffled, I read the description of the site:

"Emma Frost is an egotistical greedy twit, who doesn't know when to stop. Her editors are monkeys, she thinks she's all that, and she ruins everything. Join this group if you feel the same way about this completely egotistical woman."

I scoffed, then read the information about the site. Under personal information, it said: *Emma Frost should go jump in a lake, along with her enormous ego and her terrible books.* Under personal interests, it said: *Emma Frost is a moron. She makes money out of other people's tragedies and deaths. She's a vulture.*

"I'm so sorry," Sophia said. "I received a friend request earlier today from this site. That's how I saw it."

I looked at Sophia and shrugged. "It's very childish, really. No one's gonna care about what they write. I know I don't."

"Well, someone seems to care," she said, and pointed to the top of the site that showed the number of followers the site had.

"Wow, one hundred and seventy-nine followers?" I said, startled.

"The page was just created yesterday," Sophia said.

"How can this be?" I tried hard to suppress the emotions going through me at that moment. I thought I was well-liked? I knew there would always be some people out there who didn't like what you did, especially as a writer. But hating me? That was a difficult pill to swallow.

Sophia went back to the front page and pointed at the first post made by the creator of the page. It was a story about me, of course, and how I had illegally hacked into the police's database to look into case files in order to get material for my books. I swallowed hard and looked at Sophia. That was some pretty serious stuff. How could this person know this about me? No one except the people closest to me knew.

"There's more," Sophia said. "It's been quoted in all the big newspapers online this morning. This could get ugly."

22

NOVEMBER 2014

They came for him while he was still in school. Rasmus saw them from the window as they crossed the courtyard outside the old building of Nordby High School. He knew who they were. Officers Morten Bredballe and Allan Jorgensen. Their faces were serious as they walked towards the front entrance of the high school. Mrs. Nygaard had her back turned to her students while scribbling on the whiteboard. Rasmus had no idea what she was talking about, and he didn't care. He hadn't cared for a long time about anything in school. It didn't matter. Nothing mattered. It was all the same crap anyway. Growing up was bogus. Adults couldn't be trusted. Was he supposed to grow up and turn into one of them? There was no way. When he looked at his parents, he saw nothing but miserable people. It wasn't worth it anyway. No, Rasmus didn't want any part of it. He didn't want to end up like them or like any of all those pathetic adults he was surrounded by.

For years, Rasmus had walked around with a knot in his stomach... constantly worried about his mother. As a child, he remembered crying in school because he was certain his mother would die before he came home from school. He remembered the fear inside of him because he never knew what his dad might do to her. It could be little things that set him off. Like Rasmus opening the door to the car into a hedge or pulling the handle too roughly on the door. His dad would yell at him for days, then turn on his mother and start yelling at her. Soon, he would be throwing things and slapping her around. It was always set off by something Rasmus did, and therefore, he always blamed himself. Growing up, he was constantly terrified of doing anything wrong. He would tiptoe around the house, making sure he didn't make a sound to set off his dad's anger. But still, it kept happening, over and over again. His dad would even pull him out of his room and put him in front of his mother so he could see what he had done to her. The bruises on her face told him he had been bad, that he had done wrong. Then he would fall to his knees and cry and apologize and promise to never do anything wrong again.

But he could never manage it. There would always be something. When he did the dishes, he might put a plate down too hard on the table. Or he might not have washed his hands properly before dinner, or he might touch the door with wet hands *trying to destroy it*. It wasn't until his teenage years that he realized there would always be something...that no matter how hard he tried, he would never be able to be quiet enough or behave correctly in the eyes of his father.

That was when he decided he needed to get away. Nobody wanted him around anyway. No one except Slender Man.

He had come to him a few months ago...inside *Minecraft*, his favorite game. At first, Rasmus had been scared of him, but soon he realized that Slender Man didn't want to harm him. He had taken part in Rasmus' game and adopted him along with others. He told him he was going to take good care of him and that he wanted him. He liked him. He made Rasmus feel like he was worth something, like he was wanted, and then he had told him to do something for him in return. Rasmus hadn't hesitated for one second. Not when Slender Man had explained why it had to be done. It made sense. It gave Rasmus a purpose in life. But he knew the officers coming for him would never understand. That's why he decided to keep quiet about everything.

They were coming to question him, but he wasn't going to give them anything. He had wondered if he should run, get away, but there was nowhere to run. He didn't have any money, and had nowhere to go. Besides, he wasn't alone in this. Slender Man would take care of him. He had impressed him. That was what he had told him after he had done it. Rasmus had never impressed anyone before. It felt good, and he wanted to keep impressing him.

The door to the classroom opened, and the principal stepped inside, followed by the two officers. They talked to Mrs. Nygaard with low voices and she looked down at Rasmus.

"Rasmus?" she said.

He looked at her.

"Pack your stuff. These gentlemen have some questions for you to answer. You have to go with them."

Rasmus had already packed everything and put on his jacket. He stood up and walked towards them. As he left the class, all the students of the school had their noses pressed against the windows. He didn't care about them. Just as he was about to get into the police car, he looked between the trees of the small forest across from the school. In there, between the trees, he was certain he spotted him... that he saw Slender Man there. Rasmus touched his nose and realized it was bleeding heavily. Rasmus wiped it away with his sleeve, then smiled and got inside the car while singing to himself:

Someone's always watching me
Someone's always there
When I'm sleeping he just waits,
and he stares

23

NOVEMBER 2014

Lisa Rasmussen couldn't believe her luck. The mayor was gone. Dead in a fire last night. A fire-arson set by some man in a suit. She couldn't have done it better herself. But it wasn't her, and that was almost the best part of it. She had thought about it many times, yes. But someone else had beaten her to it. Now, she had no opponent for the election, unless someone decided to run at the last minute, that was, but that was very unlikely. And, even if they did, they would be completely unknown to the public, and no one would vote for them.

She decided to celebrate by having an organic wheat berry tabouli salad for lunch at Café Mimosa downtown. She even bought a kale and parsley-smoothie to top it off. It was a celebration, but she still needed to stay strong and healthy.

Lisa was reading the local paper online with much satisfaction, devouring everything they had written about the death of the mayor. She tried hard to not seem too cheerful as she read about how he was killed in the fire and how his wife made it out just in time. Lisa had no idea who this guy in the suit was, but she owed him one.

"Now, it's important that you show your support and grief over the loss," her campaign manager had said when she called that morning.

"This is a major opportunity for you to show the people your human side, your soft side. You have to express your sadness in the papers and give a heck of a speech at his funeral. I'll write some words if you need me to."

Lisa knew she was right. Now it was time for her to show that side of her, even though it was hard. She wasn't sure she had it in her. Even if she was the only candidate, and she was sure to take the seat, there would still be an election. People still had to like her. She scrolled through the online articles in the national newspapers. The death of the mayor on the small island wasn't big news, but it was mentioned in most of them. But something else out of the island was a big story. The story of that writer, that Emma Frost-character. Lisa read and devoured the story about Emma Frost using illegal methods to research for her books. This was certainly interesting.

"Are you done with this? Do you want me to take your plate?" The waitress, Julia, asked.

Lisa looked up and smiled. Julia smiled back. She was very fond of Lisa, ever since Lisa had killed that serial murderer in her café a year ago.

"I'm done. Thank you."

"So, you're going to be the mayor now, huh?" she asked.

Lisa smiled her election-smile. She liked that thought. She liked it a lot. "Yes. Yes, I guess I am." She paused, remembering what her campaign manager had told her. Her face turned grave. "But, what a tragedy. I feel so sorry for poor Mrs. Bang. I'm sad that these are the circumstances in which I'll take over the seat as mayor. It will be with a heavy and grieving heart."

My God, she sounded real statesmanlike. Almost presidential. Well, what do you know? She did have it in her after all. The words didn't feel natural, but they fell at the right time. She could tell by the look on Julia's face.

"That's not your fault. I, for one, am looking forward to having you as mayor. I think you can do many great things for the island."

"Well, thank you so much."

"Could I interest you in a dessert?"

Lisa shook her head. "No. Must stay in shape. Election is coming up."

"It's chocolate cake. Organic, naturally."

It did sound interesting, but Lisa had her doubts. She couldn't allow herself to slack off now. She had to stay on course and not show any weaknesses.

"No. I'm sorry."

Julia smiled and put the plate onto her tray. "Well, maybe next time then."

Lisa gathered her things and put her iPad back in her briefcase. She had a busy afternoon ahead of her, with many important meetings. As she received the bill and signed the receipt, she started tasting the words.

"Mrs. Mayor. Mayor Rasmussen. Mayor Lisa Rasmussen. Mrs. Mayor Lisa Rasmussen."

It all had such a good ring to it, she thought to herself, as she paid her bill and got up. This was what they would call her soon. This was how she would sign her papers. As the mayor of the entire island. She was exactly what this town needed. And no one could stop her now.

24

NOVEMBER 2014

I couldn't stop reading the articles, even though Sophia told me to let it go. Once she had left, and we had drunk too much coffee and eaten an entire box of chocolate, I grabbed my laptop and went through the newspapers, trying to figure out what everyone was writing about me. It was in all the papers by noon, and one of them even wrote that people ought to stop buying my books, since they had come to be by using illegal methods. It was unethical. Another wrote that the police needed to start an investigation. I read everything, and realized that whoever had written the article on the Facebook page in the first place seemed like he had pretty thorough documentation. He had taken parts of my books and details from them and asked the police if those things had been in the media or ever been mentioned publicly. The amount of details and insider knowledge could in no way have been obtained without seeing the case-files, he stated. Furthermore, he claimed to have solid proof that he was willing to provide to the police. I couldn't help wondering what solid proof that could be? Was he himself some sort of hacker and had he traced my IP address? How the heck did he know all this?

I decided to leave it alone and got up from my chair. I poured myself another coffee and found a candy bar that I ate in one bite. I felt sorry for myself. The Facebook page had almost two hundred followers by now. Were there really so many people who hated me? I didn't like the thought. I called Morten and told him everything. I even cried a little.

"Calm down, sweetheart," he said. "We'll figure it out. But I did warn you about it. It's not something that the chief of police will look upon lightly. I just got off the phone with him and he told us to look into the matter. I tried to tell him it was just a smear campaign, but he wants us to confiscate your computer. I bought you some time by telling him that we didn't have the resources for that just yet, since we had a double homicide going on, and that took all of our time. Hopefully, he'll leave it for now, but it did sound like it was a pressing matter. Like there was someone higher up trying to get him to react to this. It's not good, Emma, but you already knew that."

I hung up, feeling slightly nervous about the whole thing. While chewing on another candy bar, I thought about Mrs. Bang and how she had lost everything, and decided this was a small problem compared to what she was going through. I still had my family and, like everything else, this would blow over at some point too.

I sat down at the laptop again, still wondering about Mrs. Bang and what she had said while sitting in Jack's fire truck. The guy who had set the house on fire had no face and was wearing a black suit and tie. He was tall and skinny. Where had I heard about that before? It rang a bell of some sort, but I couldn't wrap my head around it. I tapped the keyboard and googled it. I used keywords such as *skinny tall man suit and black tie*. More than four million results came up. I looked at the first page. They were mostly sites selling clothes for big and tall men, a list of top five mistakes men make when wearing ties, and seven rules for skinny ties. Finally, at the bottom of the first page, something appeared that looked interesting. A page in Wikipedia about someone called Slender Man. I clicked it and started reading.

Later that night, when Morten came for dinner and the kids had gone to bed, I brought it up.

"I read this today," I said, and showed him the screen. "You might want to take a look at it."

"Slender Man?" Morten looked tired. "What's that?"

"It's like this Internet creation, a legend or a myth, if you like. According to an article I read in *The Washington Post,* it's an invented character who can be traced back to an obscure forum where, in 2009, some users Photoshopped old pictures and improvised a backstory for their creations. He is depicted as a thin, unnaturally tall man with tentacle-like arms, a blank and usually featureless face, wearing a black suit. Stories of Slender Man commonly feature him stalking, abducting, or traumatizing people. The stories about him tend to change, depending on who is writing them. But, in most stories, he abducts children by making them like him, by watching them, and persuading them to do things for him. To please him. Proximity to Slender Man is often said to trigger a 'Slender sickness,' a rapid onset of paranoia, nightmares, and delusions, accompanied by nosebleeds. There are lullabies written about him and so on. It's a whole world we don't know anything about. It's like they almost worship him."

"Wait, now I remember something. Wasn't there a case, a murder in the States once that was inspired by this Slender Guy?"

"Slender Man," I corrected him. "But, yes. I was getting to that. On May 31, 2014, two twelve-year old girls in Wisconsin held down and stabbed a classmate nineteen times. And get this. When questioned later by authorities, they reportedly claimed that they wished to commit a murder as a first step to becoming *proxies*—kind of like acolytes of Slender Man. They had read about it online. One of the girls said Slender Man watched her, can read minds, and teleport. She was later found incompetent to stand trial, and her prosecution was suspended until her condition improved."

"So they tried to kill their friend as some sort of tribute to this Slender Guy?" Morten asked.

"Man. And yes. You could say that. They wanted to impress him. They said they wanted to prove that Slender Man was real."

"So, you think this has something to do with the killing of Mayor

Bang, is that it?" Morten asked with a yawn. I could tell he thought it was too far out.

"I don't know. It just sounds like him, right? The description Mrs. Bang gave in the truck."

Morten leaned back on the sofa with his arms around his head. "I don't know, Emma. It sounds a little out there, don't you think?"

I shrugged. "Maybe. I just thought that maybe this killer was somehow inspired by this Slender Man. You think that Lisa character could be behind it? Maybe dressing up so she wouldn't be recognized?"

Morten chuckled. "That's a conspiracy theory alright. Come on. Why would she kill someone? To win the mayoral election? It's not the president we're talking about here. It's the mayor of an island with a total population of three thousand people. It's hardly that attractive. Why do you think there have been no opponents to Erling Bang for years? Because no one wants the seat. I wonder why this Lisa Rasmussen even wants it. I'm sure she doesn't want it that bad, though."

"You might be right. It does sound a little extreme."

"We took in someone today for the murder of Ulrik Larsen, by the way," Morten said.

"Yeah? Who?"

"I pulled the serial number on the hunting knife and found that it belonged to a Jens Krohn. He lives here in Nordby. Down by the DK gas station."

"Oh, yeah. I know where that is. Krohn, you say? I think his son Rasmus is in Maya's class at the high school."

"Yes. We went there to get him. The old man blamed it on his son. He told us the boy had taken the knife. We didn't believe him, of course. He was drunk and pathetic. We talked to the son for an hour or so. He told us he didn't know anything about a hunting knife, that his dad would never let him touch his things. The mother confirmed that Rasmus was never allowed even close to the dad's hunting equipment."

"So, you kept the father locked up?" I asked.

"Yes. He had to sleep it off anyway. Looked like he could use a little time to think, judging by the bruises on his wife's face."

"Oh, I hate that!" I exclaimed. "A drunk and a wife-beater."

"We talked to the principal, who told us Rasmus hadn't been able to do PE for two weeks because of a severe bruise on his back. They suspected the father had done that as well."

"How I hope you'll put him away for a long time," I said, grinding my teeth. It was one thing for him to beat his wife, but the son too? How could anyone hurt a child?

Morten shrugged. "I'm afraid we probably can't do that. It was his knife, but there were no fingerprints found on it. It could have been stolen to put the blame on him. It won't stand a trial."

25

NOVEMBER 2014

The numerologist clapped her hands in excitement. She was sitting at home, going through her recordings of Emma Frost reading her article online and freaking out about it. She had installed cameras in Emma's home many months ago and knew her every move. Oh, what a joy it was to see her this perplexed, this baffled. She had no idea what just hit her.

The numerologist grabbed Misty and put her on her lap. She caressed the rat while watching Emma opening her second candy bar. She was stress eating. It was such a wonderful sight. She was clearly in distress. It was all going according to plan. But the numerologist wasn't done yet. Yes, she had hurt Emma; yes, this would definitely end up having consequences for her one way or the other, but it was far from being enough.

The numerologist clapped her hands again. This was such a fun time. She had reached more than three hundred followers on the Facebook page. People were writing on the wall how they were appalled by Emma's methods. How she should be ashamed of herself. And, most importantly, people were so angry that they told each other to start boycotting her books.

"I threw mine into the fireplace and burned them," someone wrote.

"I'm never buying any more of her books, and I've told my daughter to get rid of those we have," another wrote.

"I can't believe she would use illegal methods just to sell more books. It's disgusting. What else might she have hacked into? Hospital journals? Private computers? Is she monitoring all of us just to create a good story?"

The numerologist read the comments with much joy. This was going better than she had hoped. A journalist had messaged her and asked if they could do an interview to know more details about what she knew. But the numerologist didn't want to talk to journalists. She loved that they printed her post and made it go viral like that, but she wasn't going to reveal who she really was. She was still visiting Emma's home in the afternoons, and today, she had the pleasure of seeing the distress on Emma's face and had even given her a few words of comfort.

"I'm sure it will all pass in a few days," she said. "They'll find someone else to bully. There will always be haters out there. Pay no attention to them."

She had said the words while repressing a smile planted on her lips by the knowledge she carried, that she was behind this smear campaign, and knowing that there was more to come.

The numerologist laughed out loud while preparing her next move. She went to the public library and used their computer. She found the right file and the email address to send it to. She had created a fake email address to send it from, so they couldn't trace it back to her. Emma Frost was a genius with a computer, but the numerologist had her skills as well. She knew enough to cover her tracks. She chuckled behind the screen as she hit the send button. She gathered her bag, with her rat comfortably sleeping inside of it, then ran to her Toyota and drove back to her small apartment. She meditated for a few hours, sitting on the small mat on the floor, but it was hard to clear her head properly. So many thoughts flickered through her mind. She kept getting up and looking at the computer, wondering if the email had been opened, wondering what the reaction was going to be. What if he ignored the email? What if he didn't click the link?

Stop it. You're being paranoid. Of course he will. Relax. It'll be fine. The numbers are with you. The universe and stars aligned. It couldn't be a more perfect time. Remember, November is the month everything will change. The numbers told you. Remember the five in the upper right side of the pyramid.

The numerologist closed her eyes and sighed deeply, feeling relaxed. Yes, it was all going to go exactly as planned. Nothing could stop her now.

Five was her number. The number of change. The number of death.

26

NOVEMBER 2014

The phone wouldn't stop ringing the following day. Journalists from every media outlet wanted to ask me if the accusations against me were true, if I wanted to make a statement. I told them I wasn't interested in talking to anyone. I knew I would come off as guilty, but then again, I was guilty. I had done those things. I had hacked the police files, I had hacked into private bank accounts, and I had hacked the government. I had even, at one point, hacked into the national social security register, the register that contained everything there was to know about everyone in the country. It was a felony, and not one looked upon lightly. I had known it all along, but never thought I'd get caught. I was very careful. My ex-boyfriend had taught me everything I knew, and especially how to not get caught. I couldn't believe someone had tracked me anyway. The question was whether they had the proof they claimed to have? Or if it was all just a bluff. If they had something solid, would it be enough to have me convicted? If so, I could face up to years in prison for this. It was sensitive informa-tion I was messing with. I had no idea how much they knew. I stared at my laptop and wondered what to do. It wouldn't be long before they demanded to take it. It contained all the information and would reveal just how busy I had been.

I had to get rid of it.

I felt awful. This computer had been with me for years. But it was also evidence. I opened the cover and started transferring all the data, including all my books, to a micro SD card. I ran a program to wipe the hard drive clean, but wasn't sure it was enough. I knew there were still ways to recover the data. I couldn't risk that. I hid the SD card inside a hollow wooden chesspiece in my living room, then took the computer outside and smashed it onto the tiles on my back porch. I found a hammer and started smashing it to pieces. Kenneth circled me, barking, then grabbed a letter from the keyboard that sprang loose and ran away with it.

"Don't eat that, Kenneth!"

The dog kept running and hid among the trees. I ran after him and fought him to get the piece out of his mouth.

"You'll choke on this," I said, showing it to him once I had won the battle. "Annoying as you might be, my daughter really likes you, so I intend to keep you around for a little longer."

I had just gotten back to the remains of the computer when I heard a car drive up in front of the house. I looked through the windows of the house and saw a big black van drive into my driveway on the other side. I had a bad feeling about it.

Frantically, I attacked the computer with the hammer and smashed it into bits and pieces, but I wasn't sure it was enough. I was afraid they might be able to get to the hard drive anyway. I pulled the hard drive out and smashed it with the hammer, while hearing someone knocking hard on my front door. The hard drive cracked, but didn't seem to break. I heard voices yelling and more knocking, then I spotted a small can of lighter gas next to the barbeque grill. I poured it on top of the remains of the computer, then lit it on fire. The fire crackled and it smelled awful, but it melted fast. Soon, the hard drive turned into liquid piles of molten goo.

Seconds later, some guy in a suit stormed into the house and soon spotted me on the porch. Three other guys, also wearing suits, flanked him. They looked like they had just stepped out of a movie about secret agents or the FBI.

"Outside," one of them yelled.

The first guy came out. He showed me his badge. It looked different that Morten's. "PE," he said.

I swallowed hard. The National Police Intelligence Force, *Politiet's Efterretningstjeneste?* Here? In my backyard? It was surreal.

They stared at the computer on the tiles, or what was left of it. I tried to smile, but it came off awkward.

"My computer caught on fire while I was using it. It was old. Probably the battery or maybe I used the wrong charger, huh?"

The man looked seriously at me. "That's evidence. Destroying evidence is a serious offense."

"Is it evidence? Ah, well I'm sorry, but it just caught on fire accidentally a few minutes ago. I was lucky I managed to get it outside before it burned down the entire house, huh? Real lucky. Phew. Boy..."

The man looked at his three colleagues. "We'll take it in anyway."

The three guys started picking up whatever was left. The man who had spoken came close to me. "Do you have any other computers in the house?"

"Only my daughter's upstairs, but that's..."

He lifted a hand to shut me up. "We'll take that one as well."

"You can't do that. My daughter has all her stuff on it. She'll kill me. She needs it for homework."

"She'll have to manage without."

"Come on, guys! She's just a teenager. You know how they are. They play *Minecraft*, use Facebook, Twitter, and Instagram. They can't live without their computers."

"As I said. She'll have to manage. Our orders are to remove every computer from this house. So, that's what we'll do."

27

NOVEMBER 2014

"**T**HEY TOOK ALL THE COMPUTERS?"

Morten sounded as surprised as I was. I was holding the phone to my ear as I watched the men in suits put Maya's computer into their van and take off. I felt violated somehow, like they were robbing me, invading my private life. I hated the way they looked at me, like I was some criminal.

Which I was, of course.

"Yes, but luckily mine had caught on fire before they got here," I said. I felt paranoid and didn't want to tell him what had really happened over the phone, in case they were listening in on this conversation. If PE was involved, anything could happen.

"It caught on fire? How?" Morten sounded confused.

"I'll tell you later," I said. "But they took the remains and Maya's computer. They told me I couldn't even go close to a computer for a long time, since there was an investigation going on. I can't even go to the library, they said. If I use a computer, they'll lock me up." I was about to cry as I spoke. I felt such a mixture of emotions. Anger was definitely among them, but I was also nervous and scared.

"What will they do to me? Could I go to jail for this?" I asked.

Morten exhaled. "I don't know, Emma. It's pretty serious stuff. They just sentenced a guy to four years in prison for doing something similar."

My heart dropped. "I read about that case. It was a Danish guy and some Swedish guy, right?"

"Yep. They broke into the police files and the social security register. Didn't steal anything or do anything, but breaking in is enough."

I leaned on the counter in my kitchen. I felt so bad. I had always thought it was all right since I had good intentions, since I did it to gather information about and help solve cases, but they didn't know that. They didn't care what my intentions were. Breaking in was breaking in. A crime was a crime. I had even broken into people's bank accounts. Not to steal, but that didn't matter. I could have stolen from them if I wanted to.

"I feel terrible," I said.

"I'm sure things will work out, but for now, lay low, okay? Don't do anything stupid. And whatever you do, stay away from computers. Promise me that."

"How am I supposed to work? I've already passed the deadline for my next book. What do I do?"

"Call your editor and tell her everything, then call your lawyer and find out your options. Now, I have to run. Busy day around here. We have a missing person's report this morning. A Laiyla Ejlersen is missing. Her mother was here to tell us. We have to go and talk to her husband later. Her mother thinks he killed her. Probably nothing, but we have to check it out."

"Did you ever find the owner of that bike in the bushes at Mayor Bang's house?" I asked.

"Sure. It belonged to some kid named William Korsvig. He's some high-school kid. We gave it back to him. He told us it had been stolen the other night."

"I know him. He's in Maya's school too. He was in her class last year, but was held back a year because he was absent too much. His mom remarried two years ago, Maya told me. She liked him, but he turned so angry when the step-dad moved in, and he cut off all of his friends. She told me she felt so sorry for him because the step-dad didn't care much about him, nor did his mother since his step-dad had moved in. Do you think he had something to do with the fire?"

"No. That's ridiculous," Morten said.

Thoughts flickered through my mind. I couldn't wrap my head around them, but something was wrong here, my gut told me. "It's just a little strange that two teenage boys would turn up in this investigation, don't you think?"

Morten sighed. I knew he was closing his eyes and rubbing his forehead, like he always did when he was tired and annoyed. "No, Emma. I don't think so. We don't even know if the two deaths are in any way related. After all, the mayor had his share of enemies, people that wanted him removed from his post. Kind of comes with the territory. Not everything he's done has been popular around here. No, there's nothing that indicates that the two deaths are related. They are two very different methods of killing. I think you're seeing ghosts, Emma."

"That might be...but..."

Morten interrupted me. "Focus on getting your own stuff in order now, Emma. I'll focus on the police work. Please, just promise me you'll stay out of trouble."

"I'll try," I said and hung up, knowing very well that there was no way I could keep that promise.

28

NOVEMBER 2014

They met at the old lighthouse on the tip of the island. No one would see them this time of year when there were almost no tourists. The wind blew hard from the North Sea and made the tips of their noses red. They didn't hug or shake hands when they met. All they did was exchange looks, then turn to stare at the raging ocean beneath them.

"I was surprised you called," Peter Larsen said.

He had changed a lot since back then, Jonna Frederiksen thought. He looked like an old man now. He was wearing a leather jacket with a big eagle on the back and the letters HA on it. Jonna knew what it meant. Peter had been in the Hell's Angels for many years now. It was his choice. He had made a lot of strange choices in his life since their ways parted many years ago.

"I thought it was important," she said.

"I guess," Peter said. His long silver hair was caught by the strong wind. Jonna observed him closely. He was still quite handsome. Always had been. But it hadn't been him she had loved. It had been his brother. Her first great love.

"I guess you heard he's gone," Peter said.

Jonna pulled up the hood of her long coat. She thought about how wonderful her life had been back then. How beautiful everything had been. The sky, the clouds, even the trees seemed to have been more colorful back then.

"I did. I'm so sorry..."

Peter shook his head. "Don't be. It won't change anything."

"No, I'm sorry he died before you made up with him. He did what he did for you, you know." Jonna said, insisting. She was looking at Peter now. He seemed just like the spoiled kid he had been back then...not understanding his brother's love, how far it went and how deep it was.

"I know," Peter said. "I know he did what he felt like he had to do. But that doesn't make it right."

"What he protected you from wasn't right, Peter. You must know that." Jonna said. She sighed. This wasn't why they were supposed to meet. They hadn't spoken in almost half a century. It wasn't a time to be arguing about the past.

"What he did was wrong. He made many bad choices that I can't forgive," Peter said.

"Let's not argue," Jonna said. "We're the only two left."

"I know. Erling died in that fire." Peter shook his head. "He was a good mayor for many years."

"Do you think there's a connection?" Jonna asked.

Peter sucked in air through his teeth. "I'd be lying if I said I haven't thought about it."

"Me too. But who? Who would know?" she asked.

Peter shrugged. "I have no idea. But it is strange."

They both went very quiet. The silence was tough on both of them, since they knew what the other was thinking.

Could I be next?

"So, what should we do?" Jonna asked. "Do you have any suggestions?"

"I'm getting out of here," Peter said. "Taking the ferry first thing in the morning. Should have done it many years ago. This island has too many bad memories."

"Where will you go?" Jonna asked.

He shrugged again. "Anywhere and everywhere. Ride my motorcycle into the unknown. Ride till I can't anymore. I've always dreamt of touring around Europe. Just keep going till I run out of cash."

Jonna looked out at the ocean. The waves were crashing the shore. The ocean looked almost black. She could have sworn it hissed at her and reminded her of what she had done.

She nodded calmly. There was no way she could do the same. She was strong and agile, but she could never leave this island. No matter how bad things got, she simply had to live with it. She had to manage. And if someone came for her, then well...she'd simply have to defend herself, even if it meant she'd lose. Besides, there was something else she wanted to do before she left this earth, something she had always dreamt of. And that involved staying on the island.

She thought about shaking his hand, but knew he hated her as much as he had hated his brother for their actions back then.

"Well, God's speed then. Travel safe," she said, and took one last glance at his beautiful face, remembering those joyful times back then with his brother.

"Thanks."

29

NOVEMBER 2014

"**THEY TOOK MY COMPUTER?**"

Maya looked like it was something I had decided, like it was all my fault. She had just come home from school and thrown her bag in the hallway when I told her.

"I'm sorry, sweetie. I couldn't help it. It was the Police Intelligence Force. Do you have any idea how serious that is?"

Maya scoffed. "But...but...couldn't you just have said no?"

"You don't say no to these people, believe me," I said, trying to sound like it was no big deal. "You'll get it back as soon as they're done with it."

"But..." Maya's cheeks had turned red. I could tell she wanted to yell at me.

"It's not my fault," I said.

"But they took it because of what you've done, right?" she asked. "Because they think you've been hacking. Don't you think I know that? Don't you think everyone is talking about you in school? It is so embarrassing, Mom!"

"I'm sorry, Maya, but there isn't much I can do about it." I looked at the kitchen table. I had set it all up for when the kids got home.

Being without a computer gave me a lot of extra time. I had even cleaned all the bathrooms upstairs.

"I made hot chocolate. Come and sit. I even baked a cake. Carrot cake. Your favorite."

"That's not my favorite," she snarled.

"Is it Victor's then? I can't remember. But I'm sure you'll like it. Come, have a piece. Everything will look much brighter after a piece of cake and hot chocolate. Victor should be home in a few seconds as well."

Maya looked like she was about to explode. "I need that computer!"

"And I would gladly buy you a new one if I was allowed to. But I can't go anywhere near a computer until they're done with the investigation."

Maya stomped her feet on the kitchen floor, then ran up the stairs and slammed her door. I heard music thumping seconds later.

I felt agitated and upset, so I sat down and had just cut myself a piece of the cake when Victor came in.

"Hi, buddy. Just in time. I made your favorite cake," I said.

"Where's Brutus?" he said. Ever since we got that dog, it was all he ever talked about or even looked at. I was air to him.

"Probably sitting in the living room, as usual," I said, and took a bite of my cake.

"I need to take him for a walk."

I shrugged while giving up being able to eat together as a family. "Knock yourself out," I said. "Cake will still be here when you return."

Victor left to take care of Brutus, while Kenneth was gnawing on one of the legs of my chair. He was growling as he tore the wood into pieces. I didn't even bother trying to stop him. I sighed and drank my coffee, feeling a little lost. Without being able to write, I was bored, to put it mildly. I loved my job. I loved snooping around on the Internet. Heck, I loved going on Facebook and reading all the crap people posted.

They didn't say anything about my iPad, did they?

I ate another piece of my cake while shaking my head. No, they had only said computer. They had only taken our computers, not our phones or my iPad. Well, I didn't actually tell them I had one. They hadn't asked either. So, did that mean I was allowed to access the Internet on them? I decided it did. I walked to the living room, grabbed my iPad from the drawer and went back to the kitchen, just as Sophia stormed in. I knew something was wrong just by the look on her face.

"Have you seen it?"

I shrugged. "I guess not. I mean I've seen a lot lately, but try me," I said and sat down.

"Where's your computer?" she asked and looked at where my laptop used to be.

"Taken, burned, whichever you prefer."

She shook her head, looking baffled. "What?"

"Long story. PE was here. The computer caught on fire. Not in that order, but to get to the point, it's gone. The computer is gone. PE took Maya's as well."

Sophia looked at the iPad in my hands. "But you still have your iPad; that's good. Log onto Facebook. I need to show you something."

I tapped on the iPad, when I heard a noise by the door. It opened and Morten stepped in. I looked at the clock on the wall.

"What are you doing here this early? Has something happened?"

Sophia looked shocked. "I was too late," she said.

Morten hung his head. Then he nodded.

I looked from one to the other. "Would anyone mind letting me know what the hell is going on here?"

30

NOVEMBER 2014

"They suspended me from the force."

Morten sat down at the table; Sophia had poured him a cup of coffee that he didn't touch. I hadn't seen him in this much distress before. It scared me like crazy.

"But why?" I asked. "What happened?"

"I...I..." Morten looked at me. His voice was breaking. "I'm not sure I even understand it myself."

"It was that page again, Emma," Sophia said. "That Facebook page. I was trying to tell you. I came over as soon as I read it."

I felt the blood boiling inside of me. "They wrote something that hurt Morten and got him suspended?" I asked.

"Yes." Sophia turned the iPad and showed me. A picture of Morten was on the wall, the text underneath saying:

EMMA FROST'S BOYFRIEND A SICK PERVERT?

I looked at Sophia. "Do I even want to read this?"

Morten shook his head. "Don't. I don't want you to read it."

"Just tell me what it says," I said and sipped my coffee.

"We need something stronger for this," Sophia said and got to her feet. She pulled out the old whiskey that we only drank when she was around. She put some in all of our coffees. I sipped mine again and felt the alcohol burn my throat. Morten drank all of his and asked for more.

"Okay. Break it to me gently," I said. "What have the bastards written about you? All lies, I suppose."

Morten tilted his head. "Well...not exactly."

"What?"

"I opened an email," he said. "It contained a link. I thought it was harmless, but there were animals in it. They were being...well they were..."

"Raped by humans," Sophia said. "It was porn. At least according to the article on Facebook."

I almost choked on the coffee. "What? Why would you be looking at that kind of stuff?"

"I had no idea what it was. But apparently, the video was downloaded to my work computer and I didn't know. It's illegal to download that kind of movie, so now I might be charged with possession of illegal porn. And I was suspended until they can look into the matter."

I leaned back in the chair. "I...I don't know what to say to this. I'm completely baffled. It's so surreal that all of this is happening to us. Someone is out to ruin us, to destroy us. And he's succeeding, isn't he?"

"It looks like it," Sophia said. "People are writing some ugly stuff about you online. I won't go into the details, but it's not very nice."

"And it's hurting my book sales. My publisher called earlier and told me several of the bookstores have sent my books back, since they can't sell them anymore or won't because of the ethical stuff, the way they were created. Can you believe this?" I asked looking at them both. "Who the hell is behind this?"

"I don't know," Sophia said. "It's so easy to be anonymous these days. Online, you can say anything you like without having to answer to anyone. It's really ugly."

I looked at Morten, who looked so incredibly ashamed. "And you.

Why on earth would you open a link like that? Why would you click on it?"

"I...the email came from you," he said. "It said in the email that it was something cute I had to see, so I clicked on it."

"I never send emails like that, and I'd certainly never send that one."

"It came from EmmaFrost12@hotmail.com, so I assumed you had stumbled onto something that you wanted me to see."

"First of all, I've had no computer all day..."

"It was this morning. The email was sent last night," Morten argued.

"Okay. But that's not my email address. I use Gmail. You know that."

Morten shrugged. "Well, I do now. To be honest, I didn't notice it was a Hotmail address till afterwards. I just saw your name."

"And by then, it was too late," I said.

31

APRIL 1964

Dear Sister,

I am sorry that it has been so long since my last letter. Things have been busy here at the farm. You wouldn't believe how big the boys are now. Ulrik is turning eighteen this fall, Peter just turned sixteen, and Per is five years old now. Oh, how time flies. You wouldn't believe it.

Ulrik is working full time on the farm with Claes now, and has been since he finished ninth grade two years ago. He wanted to go to high school like the other children, he said, but Claes wouldn't hear of it. The boy is going to be a farmer and doesn't need to read books, he said. I guess he's right. It is just difficult when you know your son really likes to read books and actually enjoys school. I thought about talking to Claes about letting Ulrik go to high school and let Peter take over the farm instead, since Peter loves working with his hands and can't wait to get out of school. But that's not the way Claes wants it to be. The oldest takes over the farm, just like he himself took over from his father. He is very firm on that, and I can't argue with him.

But it is difficult as a mother to see your son look at his brother with longing jealous eyes as he takes his bike and rides it to school every morning. Per will start school next year as well, and then Ulrik will be the only kid left at the farm all day. It's going to be tough on him. He doesn't seem to enjoy this work much, nor does he seem to look forward to his future here on the farm. I worry about him a lot, but you probably know how that is, having a son of your own.

Since Ulrik is working full time here now, there isn't much work for Peter to do once he gets out of school, so our neighbor, old Hansen, is paying him to work on his farm every weekend. I do think Peter will be the one using his hands for a living. He is very skilled in almost all areas of handiwork, especially when it comes to carpentry. That is where his real skills lie. He has built an entire new barn for Old Mr. Hansen and helped put a new roof on his house. Peter certainly will do well in this life, I am sure.

Our youngest, Per, is still the one bringing me the most joy. He is such a happy child. Oh, sister, I wish you could come and visit again soon and see how big he is now and experience how wonderful a boy he has turned out to be. Everyone loves being in his company and he always makes me laugh. He has a way with animals. You should see him with the dogs. He plays with them and trains them to do all kinds of tricks. He likes the outdoor life and spends most of his time with the animals. He rides our horses and they seem to obey his every command. It's truly amazing. He even adores the pigs and has named all of them, even though I've told him that he really shouldn't, since they're meant to be slaughtered eventually. He doesn't seem to care. I'm curious how he will take it once he has to start school in the fall. He'll be devastated to not be able to spend time with the animals all day. Well, it's the way it must go, I guess. He'll grow up and be a blessing to this world. I'm sure of it. He's such a beautiful boy. Such a delight to be around. Never gets himself in trouble. Nothing like his older brothers. I still consider him my baby, but I guess it will always be like that with your youngest.

How are things in the city? Is Bengt still doing well in school? I will try and see if I can come for a visit in the fall if Claes permits it. He seems to think we have more important things to do than go to the city. I try and tell him I would like to see something different for once. I'm tired of cornfields and pigsties. We will harvest the wheat in August...that's the busiest time of the year for us. Maybe I will find the time to come for a visit in September or October. I can't believe it has been almost three years since we last saw each other. Where does the time go?

With love,
Helle

32

NOVEMBER 2014

I put the letter back in the envelope and into the box. I stared at the iPad on the table. Morten was walking around upstairs. He hadn't been able to rest all afternoon. Neither had I, and I thought reading one of my grandmother's letters would make me forget my troubles. I had succeeded for a little while, but now it was all back again. I felt a knot in my stomach, and it wasn't because of the carrot cake that I had finished all by myself; it was because of the uncertainty, the anxiety for the both of us. What was this going to mean for us?

I had called my lawyer, Helene Quist, and she promised to look into the matter. She asked me to send her an email with all the information. I couldn't help laughing.

"I'm not allowed near a computer," I said, still chuckling.

"Oh. I forgot. Well then, I'll call PE and tell them they'll have to go through me from now on, and have them send over the charges against you. We'll get to the bottom of this. Don't you worry."

But I did. I worried like crazy, wondering if I would have to go to jail. Wondering if I would ever be able to sell a book again.

I grabbed the iPad and went online. I checked the Facebook page. Almost a thousand followers now, and lots of nasty comments on the story about me, and even more on the one about Morten. I closed the app and went online to check the newspapers. Morten's story wasn't front-page news, but they all mentioned his suspension. Only because he was my boyfriend; otherwise, they wouldn't have bothered. It annoyed me. Everything about this affair annoyed me immensely. Especially the fact that I felt paralyzed. This guy could post all these things about me and my loved ones, and I couldn't do a damn thing about it. How was that even possible? It was spreading like a fire around the web and people were getting in line to scold me. Why were people so nasty online?

So, what was I supposed to do now? Just sit here and take a beating? What else would this person come up with?

I'm not gonna just sit here and take it. The hell I am.

I got to my feet and walked to the closet in the hallway. I found a hooded sweater and a big fluffy jacket that I hardly ever used. I also found a dark-haired wig that I had bought for *Fastelavn*, but never used. I put it all on and pulled the hood over my head. I looked in the mirror, then pulled out a drawer in the dresser. I found a pair of my dad's glasses that he had forgotten when visiting one day and put them on as well. There. No one would recognize me now.

Kenneth barked at me like I was an intruder, but he always did that. I gave him an old shoe to gnaw. That should keep him busy for a little while. I yelled to Morten and Maya that I was going out for a little, then left. I walked through town in the drizzle, sensing how my steps became angrier and more powerful the more I walked. Why was this strange person behind the Facebook page so keen on hurting me? On hurting Morten? What did he get out of it? I didn't understand how anyone could act like this. It was a fair amount of work he had put into finding these accusations against us. It took a lot of work and planning to create the email and send it to Morten, not to mention all the work it took to find out in which passages in my books I had provided details that weren't known to the public. This guy was really out to get me, and I had a feeling he wasn't going to stop anytime soon.

I entered the public library, found a computer, and sat down, making sure no one spotted me. I opened Facebook and found the page that had the articles about Morten and me, then I opened Morten's Hotmail account that I knew the password for. I scrolled down and found the email allegedly sent from me.

"Someone's gone to a lot of trouble here," I mumbled. "Creating a false account in my name and everything."

I looked around to make sure no one was watching me, then started a trace to find which IP address the email had been sent from. While waiting for the result, I tapped my fingers and looked around nervously again. The librarian, Mrs. Houman, was deeply buried in the newspaper behind the counter. She paid no attention to me. Still, I constantly felt like I was being watched. But I had felt that a lot lately.

The result came up and, to my surprise, the IP address was the library, the same address that I was stationed at. In other words, whoever was behind this had used the computers at the library to send the email to Morten. He wasn't sitting behind a computer somewhere far away ruining my life. He was here on the island somewhere.

33

NOVEMBER 2014

Lisa Rasmussen felt annoyed as she parked the car in front of SuperBrugsen, the city's only supermarket. She had spent the afternoon in meetings and just got the call that one of the local police officers had turned out to be a pervert and had been suspended for being in possession of some outrageous porn. To top it off, he was Emma Frost's boyfriend, so the story was all over the online newspapers already.

Lisa sighed aggressively and looked out through the windshield. It was raining heavily now. It was dark already. On the streetlamp, her poster was getting soaked. Someone had painted a mustache on her upper lip. Lisa felt tired. Tired of this island and its people. She couldn't believe them. Didn't anyone have any respect anymore? Especially, Emma Frost annoyed her immensely. She was bad news for the island. All those stories going on right now attracted the wrong kind of attention to the island. And Lisa was trying to get the tourism back. It was her cause, the one that was going to get the islanders to love her.

Luckily, there still hadn't been another candidate announced, and she doubted that there was going to be, since there were less than two weeks till the election.

"You will be mayor, Lisa, no doubt about it. There's nothing that can stop you now. Don't worry. Just breathe," she told her own reflection in the rearview mirror. "They will come to love you. They will learn to. Or you'll make them."

Lisa closed her eyes and calmed down. All this bad publicity was getting to her. How was she supposed to fix things? How was she supposed to get people to return here? This island lived off the tourists. And it was like it kept getting worse and worse. One bad thing after the other. The news of the old man Larsen, who was killed in his home, had spread as well. So had the story of the mayor getting killed in the fire, even though they had told the newspapers it was an accident. Lisa had held a meeting with her people and asked them to figure out what to do about the island's bad reputation. If she was going to get people to elect her and love her as a mayor for bringing back the tourists and the good reputation of the island, she needed to do something extraordinary. They had to figure out what that could be. But their suggestions hadn't been useful so far.

Amateurs. Always surrounded by freaking amateurs.

Lisa took in a deep breath to calm herself down. She puffed her hair with her hands to make it look good, then put on her election smile before she exited the car. She grabbed a cart and walked through the sliding doors, smiling at everyone and nodding, even if they didn't look at her.

"Hello. Don't forget to vote," she said to as many people as possible. It was her campaign manager who had told her it was important that she was seen in public doing ordinary chores, but always with a smile and showing her best side. It was all about appearing ordinary, showing she was one of them. According to a questionnaire, that was the only problem the islanders had with her. That she wasn't local; she wasn't one of their own. They didn't like that. So now, Lisa had to show them that she was just like them. Lisa grabbed some cereal, put it in the cart, and continued down the aisle. She nodded and smiled at a couple she passed while grabbing a head of lettuce to go with the lasagna she was preparing for tonight. She hurried past the meat, since she wouldn't be needing any of that for quite awhile. She had the entire freezer full. When she stopped at the fruit section, a cart was blocking her way. A woman was bent over the apples. Lisa needed oranges and had to pass the woman to get to them, but couldn't.

She clenched her fist, but kept smiling. There was nothing more annoying than when people blocked the way with their cart and then took forever to move it. Lisa cleared her throat to let the woman know she was waiting for her. The woman didn't react. Lisa looked at her while her nostrils flared, but kept smiling. She cleared her throat again, this time a little louder. The woman still didn't react. She was touching all the apples, feeling them one after another in her hands to see if they were ripe. She even smelled some of them and had her disgusting nose touch them before she put them back. That annoyed Lisa even more. She had to address it.

"You're not supposed to touch all of them," she said.

The black-haired woman turned her head and looked at her. She was Asian. Lisa bit her lip. She had never liked Asian people much. Never trusted them. Something about their eyes just wasn't right. They had all kinds of diseases out there in the East, didn't they? Lisa had always been terrified of getting SARS or MERS, or whatever those diseases were called. Especially, bird flu scared the crap out of her. What those Asians did to those birds to get the disease, she never wanted to know.

"Excuse me?" the Asian woman asked.

Lisa wrinkled her nose. "You're touching all of them," she said. "It's gross. Don't touch those, and certainly don't put your nose on them if you're not buying them. Think about others. Besides, your cart is blocking the way so no one can pass you."

To Lisa's surprise, the Asian woman burst out into loud laughter. It was very odd, Lisa thought. Everything about this woman came off as very odd. The woman was still chuckling as she grabbed another apple and put it in her small plastic bag. "I just need one more," she said. "Then I have five. Five is my lucky number, you see."

Lisa sighed and looked at her watch. It was getting late. She had a dinner to cook. "Please, just move your cart a little," she said. "I'm in a hurry."

The Asian woman smiled from ear to ear. "I can tell," she said. "Your entire aura is completely messed up. You really should calm down a little."

Lisa snorted. "I don't have the time to calm down a little. I'm very busy, as you can see. Now, please, just move your cart."

"I could clean it for you, you know?" the woman said. "I could clean your aura. I'm guessing your life path number is all wrong for you. I could help you find a new name and completely change your life. You'll be surprised when you realize how much it means."

Lisa's eyes glowed in anger. What the heck was this? Who was this insane woman? Never had she heard anything this ridiculous.

"Listen. I have a family to get home to, that doesn't see me much, and I have a very important election coming up. I really just want to get to the oranges over there, so I can be done and go home. Do you have any idea who I am?"

"No."

Lisa stared paralyzed at the woman in front of her. She still hadn't moved her cart. She picked up her purse and Lisa noticed that there was something inside of it. A small face peered out. Lisa gasped and pointed.

"A...a rat!"

The Asian woman kissed the disgusting rat on the mouth. It returned the kiss by licking her nose before she put it back in her purse with a smile. Lisa could have thrown up right on the spot. She could hardly speak; the anger was boiling in her throat.

"You...you...brought a RAT to the supermarket? You have it near the food? You kiss it on the mouth and let it lick your nose? The same filthy nose that you use for sniffing the fruit?"

The Asian woman shrugged. "Yeah. So?"

Lisa had no more words. She was so shocked she couldn't stand being in the supermarket anymore. She grabbed the handle of her cart, then smashed it into the woman's cart several times until the cart moved sideways enough for her to get through. With a loud whimper of distress and anger, Lisa stormed past her towards the cashier, while thinking to herself:

No wonder they get all these diseases out there! Well, I'm not having it here. Not on our peaceful island. I'm not. I'm simply not tolerating it!

As she threw her groceries on the counter for the cashier to ring them up, she stared at the moving objects, still in shock, while mumbling, "I'm such a fool. We just had lasagna last week. I'll serve sausages instead."

34

NOVEMBER 2014

When I came home from the library, Morten was sitting in the kitchen. He looked upset.

"Where have you been?" he asked.

"I told you I went out for a little bit."

"You've been gone for two hours," he snarled.

"Well, I'm sorry. I didn't realize I had to hurry back," I said, and put my jacket on a hanger and put it in the closet in the hallway.

"I'm sorry," Morten said. "I'm just so frustrated. The chief of police just called and asked me to be in his office tomorrow morning. With the cutbacks we're facing, I'm pretty sure he's not going to promote me."

I grabbed a chair and sat down. "Oh, you're afraid he's going to fire you?"

"I'm not exactly popular on the force right now. Allan won't even return my calls. They all think I'm some pervert."

"I'm sure they don't think that," I said and got to my feet. "Let me make us some coffee. I think I have some butter cookies in the cabinet."

I grabbed the pot and poured water into it. Morten looked at me. "Is that your answer to everything? Food? Coffee?"

"Ouch. That hurt," I said.

Morten exhaled. He closed his eyes and rubbed his forehead. "I'm sorry. I'm not myself. I'm just so...so angry with myself. Why did I open that stupid link? Why did I click it?"

I put the pot on the coffeemaker and turned it on. Then I sat down again. I desperately wanted to indulge myself in a box of cookies to forget everything, but I restrained myself. Morten was right. Food was my answer to everything. It was becoming an awful habit.

"Anyone could have made that mistake," I said. "Don't be so hard on yourself."

"But I should have known it didn't come from you. How could I have been that stupid?" he asked.

"I don't know, sweetie. But looking back won't change a thing. We need to figure out who sent that email in the first place. We need to stop this harassment before it goes any further. I have no idea who is out to get us, but I am determined to find out and make it stop."

Morten looked up at me. "How?"

"I went to the library," I said. "I found something out. Whoever sent the email, sent it from the library's computer. It was the same IP address. That tells me he's somewhere here on the island. We can find him."

Morten looked like he couldn't believe me. "You went on a computer at the library?" he asked.

"Yes. Don't worry. I wore a disguise. No one recognized me. Besides, I was the only one there. I was very careful."

Morten looked like he might explode. "Are you INSANE?" he yelled.

"Sh. Keep your voice down. Dr. Sonnichsen is working with Maya upstairs. I saw her car in the driveway."

"Have you completely lost it?" Morten asked very loudly. He was angry now. He was furious.

"You know you're not supposed to go anywhere near a computer.

If they find out, they'll lock you up. Are you just trying to ruin everything?"

I froze. What did he just say?

"What do you mean 'ruin everything'? You think this is entirely my fault, don't you? You think I'm to blame for all this."

Morten didn't answer.

"Answer me, goddammit!" I said.

He shrugged. "Well...Yes."

I couldn't believe him. "What?"

"Well, if you hadn't hacked into the police files so often, it would have never been discovered, would it? I bet that's how they found the link on my computer. Because they were searching for material on you, to use in their case against you. So, they stumbled onto that stupid video, and now I'm going down with you."

I scoffed. "I can't believe what you're saying here. You opened that email. Even though you knew it wasn't from me. I mean, how stupid can you be to open a link like that? You brought this upon yourself. I had nothing to do with it."

"Oh, now you're finally telling the truth, huh? What happened to *it could have happened to anyone, don't be so hard on yourself*? Huh? Was that just another of your acts?"

I looked at him feeling tears piling up. What was happening to us? "Morten..." I said, and reached out my hand to touch his arm, but he pulled it away. "Morten, do you want..."

He interrupted me as he got to his feet. "No, I don't want anymore STUPID cake or candy or coffee or buns or whatever you want to fill me up with to make me shut up, to make us forget everything else. It might work for you, Emma, but it doesn't work on me. I'm losing my job here. I might never get to work again. And it's all your fault!" Stating the final words in a harsh tone, he stormed out and slammed the front door as he left.

35

NOVEMBER 2014

"Oh, happy day! Oh what fun we had today, didn't we, little Missy? Yes, we did! We had so much fun!"

The numerologist walked—almost danced—into her apartment and let the rat out of her purse as she walked into the kitchen and started unpacking all of her groceries. The milk was placed in the fridge first to make sure it wouldn't go bad, then the eggs and the cheese. As she pulled out the apples, she couldn't stop laughing, thinking about that woman in the supermarket and watching her upset face. What a bonus it had been to be able to tick her off like that. The numerologist knew perfectly well who she was, of course she did. It was that lady from the posters, the one running for mayor, who no longer had an opponent because the mayor had been killed. But it had been a lot of fun pretending she didn't know. Just seeing the look on the woman's face was priceless.

"Yes, she was the crazy one, wasn't she Missy?" the numerologist said, as the rat came into the kitchen and crawled onto the counter. The numerologist unpacked her bags and handed the rat an apple. She sat in front of the computer while eating one herself. Juices from the apple ran down her hand. The numerologist went online to check out the newspapers. To her enjoyment, they were all over the story of the officer and boyfriend of Emma Frost who had been suspended because of some porn movie on his computer. No one asked how the police were tipped off about the movie. How did they even know to look for it?

That was between the numerologist and the chief of police in Esbjerg.

The numerologist took another big bite of her apple and slurped the juices from it, licking its sides. She stared at the articles on the screen and printed a couple of them out for her scrapbook. They were worth keeping. She was so immensely proud of herself and what she had accomplished.

While she was with Maya this afternoon at Emma Frost's house, she had felt the extreme tension. Even Maya had been frustrated and angry and had talked to the numerologist about it.

"It's just so typical that I have to be punished for my mom doing illegal stuff," she had said. "I can't believe her. I can't believe she would do those things. Why can't she just be an ordinary boring mom like everyone else? I always get dragged into her stupid problems. It's so embarrassing. Everybody in school is talking about her. Everybody knows about her. And now they'll be talking about her boyfriend too? I can't take anymore!"

The numerologist had spoken for a long time with Maya about how almost all teenagers are ashamed of their parents, but that she also believed she was entitled to be angry with both of them.

"It's very irresponsible of them to drag all of you into this," she said, while smiling widely on the inside. She couldn't believe how well her plan was working. It was even better than she had imagined. While sitting with Maya in her room, she had felt such joy listening to Emma and Morten arguing loudly downstairs. They were getting on each other's nerves. The frustration was thick...almost to boiling. She even heard Morten slam the door in anger as he left the house.

It was pure music to her ears.

Missy was done with the apple and climbed on the table. The

numerologist observed her with joy. There was nothing like Missy to make her happy. Pets were the best, weren't they?

The numerologist chuckled with delight as she thought of her next move. A shiver went down her spine. Oh, how amazing it was going to be. She could hardly wait. It was cruel. It was evil.

It was perfect.

36

NOVEMBER 2014

He had always been a quiet and easy-going kid. That was what his grandparents had always said.

"Tommy is such a good kid. Tommy always has a smile on his face. Tommy always stays out of trouble."

To most people, Tommy Malthesen was an average sixteen-year-old kid who was being raised by two loving grandparents. Tommy's dad had died in a car accident when he was five, and his mother hadn't been able to take care of him properly. So, she had given him to her parents and he had lived with them the last ten years. It had been ten good years for all of them. Especially for Tommy, who had enjoyed having a stable life, even though it meant he only saw his mother once or twice a year. He missed her and, in the beginning, it had been difficult for him to understand why she couldn't keep him, but like in all other aspects of life, Tommy had never said anything, nor had he complained. Tommy was a good boy, a straight A student at the local high school, even if he wasn't the type that anyone took any notice of. For him, life was all about staying out of sight. Making himself invisible.

That was until he saw Maya. The day he had spotted her in the school's hallway for the first time was the day his life had begun. That was when everything changed. For the first time, he no longer desired to stay invisible to the world. For the first time, he wanted to be seen. He wanted her to see him.

But she never had. He had tried to approach her on several occasions. He tried to talk to her in the cafeteria line or at the library, but she still had no idea who he was. She remained unapproachable. And, worst of all, Tommy remained invisible to her. Now he was sitting at home in his room at his grandparents' house. He was staring at the picture of Maya he had printed out from her Instagram account so that he could put it up on his wall. He touched it gently while waiting.

"It's all for you, my beautiful. I'm doing it for your sake."

There was one time she had noticed him. He had been standing in the hallway staring at her like he always did when she and her friends had walked past him. Her friend Annika had laughed and told the others that Tommy had a crush on Maya...that he was constantly eyeballing her, then she had called him *vanilla* with a loud laugh. Tommy knew what that meant. It meant he was boring and conventional. Tommy had never thought of himself as boring, but it had hurt his feelings, and he had later decided to prove them wrong, to prove to Maya that her friend wasn't right.

Tommy looked at the computer screen. He had logged in to *Minecraft* and entered the house in the server where he used to meet *him*. He was the one that had taught Tommy that he didn't have to remain invisible for the rest of his life, that he was worth something, that he was an important person and that he deserved to be seen. And he had known exactly how to do it. How to make him the talk of the town.

"Soon you'll see me, my dear Maya. Soon, you'll see my face everywhere," he mumbled, while waiting for Slender Man to appear.

It didn't take many seconds before he did. The faceless figure walked towards him, wearing his suit and tie.

Tommy smiled and wrote:

>Hello<

A few seconds passed. Then the man replied.

>Hello, my friend<

Tommy loved that he called him his friend. Tommy had no other friends, but had always wanted one. He knew it was just a character someone had created in the game, but the person behind it was his friend. He was his best friend, and best friends would go far to help each other out.

>I've got everything you told me to get< Tommy wrote.

>Excellent. Do you have any questions?<

Tommy thought for a few seconds. He had a million questions, but wasn't sure he wanted to ask them. He just wanted to make Slender Man happy; he wanted so badly to make him proud and become one of his proxies. Almost as much as he wanted to be seen by Maya. He wanted her to know his name. Know that he had done something extraordinary. And that he had done it for her sake. Because he would do anything for her. He was going to make sure she knew. He wasn't just vanilla. There was so much more to him and they would soon learn.

>No. I'm ready. Let's do it. YOLO, right? You Only Live Once<

37

NOVEMBER 2014

I was upset. No, it was more than that. I was furious. I was sad. I was frustrated. All at once. I felt like whoever was doing this to us was winning. That was the plan, wasn't it? To drive us nuts? To make us turn on each other and fight. And he was succeeding. I got a strange feeling that this was all brilliantly planned, that we were merely puppets in a show, not having any influence over what happened to us.

Why were we so stupid to fall for it? Why were we so helpless? Why were we letting this happen?

I took the dogs for their evening walk and decided to make the walk a little longer than usual. We walked through the yard and onto the beach at the end of my property. I walked for half an hour before turning around and walking back. Kenneth constantly barked at everything. He pulled on the leash, while Brutus walked steadily and quietly next to me. I was beginning to like the dog. It was nice that he was so quiet. He wasn't at all like the shelter had said. He hardly ever growled at me anymore. Only if I touched him, which I never did... well, only to put on the leash, but I could do that with hardly touching his fur. I got a feeling he liked it at our house, and especially liked being with Victor. Those two understood each other in a way I would never comprehend.

"You're not so bad, are you Brutus?" I asked into the darkness, while Kenneth pulled the leash so hard he started wheezing.

Brutus didn't even react. He kept walking next to me, completely soundless. I had no idea how such a big dog could be this quiet. He kept sneaking up on me, appearing in my room at times when I least expected it, and without the door even being open, it seemed. It freaked me out constantly. But he never hurt a fly. Not even Kenneth, even though everyone else in the house—except for Maya, naturally—wanted to hurt him, or at least make him shut up for just one second.

I felt strange as I walked with the two dogs along the beach. It was pitch dark and I couldn't see a thing; still, I felt like someone was watching me. I had felt that a lot lately, but now the feeling was very strong. My heart rate went up and I started to walk faster.

You're being paranoid, Emma. It's nothing. Besides you have the dogs with you. No one will ever dare to hurt you when you have Brutus by your side.

Kenneth stopped to pee, and I looked around in the darkness to see if I could spot anything or anyone. I had a flashlight that I used. Kenneth did a number two and I bent over to pick it up with the bag. I heard a sound behind me and turned to look. I shone the flashlight, but there was nothing there.

"Who's there?" I asked. My voice was shivering slightly.

Nothing but darkness surrounded me.

"Hello?" I asked.

It's all in your head. This entire affair is making you sick. You need to relax, or you'll lose it.

I had taken in a couple of deep breaths of sea air, then started walking again, when I was certain I heard steps right behind me. I turned fast this time and shone the flashlight, but still...no one. It was all very strange. I walked a few steps more, then turned to look again. Still nothing but sand and ocean. On the land side, several of the houses had trees leading all the way to the beach like my property had.

I wondered why they hadn't cut them down to get better views from their houses. I was keeping mine for Victor's sake, but if I didn't have him, I would have removed them immediately. Maybe people just liked their privacy. It was silly, I thought. But everyone was different. Right now, the big pine trees were making the scene extra creepy, and I walked even faster once I returned to my track. When I turned to look behind me one more time, the flashlight accidentally hit the sand where I had been walking. Then, I stopped. In the wet sand behind me, there was an extra set of footprints next to mine, like I had been walking with someone. They stopped right where I was. My heart was racing in my chest as I frantically shone the flashlight around me.

"Where are you?" I yelled. "I know you're there. Show yourself to me, you coward! Do you want to fight, huh? Is that what you want? Let's just settle this here and now! Stop watching me, stop harassing my family and me. Leave me alone!!"

As I yelled the last words, I panted in agitation and waited for the answer. But it never came. There wasn't even a sound. Kenneth barked again and started pulling the leash. Still panting in furor, I walked home.

38

NOVEMBER 2014

Peter Larsen was worried. While packing his bag, he found a picture of him and his brother from back when they were just teenagers. He touched it gently and felt a sadness come over him. So many years had passed. So many years wasted.

He hadn't had time to grieve the loss of his brother much, and there was no time now. Peter knew he had to get off this island as soon as possible. He had originally planned to leave tomorrow, but after his talk with Jonna, he knew he had to leave now. Take the last boat right after midnight. He had seen the concern in her eyes and felt it deep within his heart. The fact that both Ulrik and Erling were killed within a few days of each other was no coincidence. It couldn't be.

It was the past finally catching up to them.

Peter put the picture inside the backpack, then closed it tightly. He wasn't taking much. Just some clothes and a few personal possessions. If he needed anything else, he could buy it.

His plan was to take his bike through Germany and France, make a few stops on the way, and then end up in Bibione in Italy. It was his favorite place in the world, and he had spent many summers there with his biker-friends, bringing nothing but their bikes and a tent. It was the simple life. He needed that.

Peter hadn't had a particularly happy or quiet life. Things had been complicated. He had been complicated. At least that was what many women had told him over the years when he refused to let them in. It wasn't that he didn't want to. He had met several women over the years that he would have liked to tell everything to, that he would have loved to share his life and secrets with, but he couldn't. He simply couldn't. He had no idea how to be close to another human being. He had no idea how to be in a relationship. He didn't want to spend the night at their places; he didn't want to leave a toothbrush. Some stayed with him for up till three years before they finally grew tired of his lack of commitment. He couldn't blame them for leaving.

Peter grabbed his leather jacket from the closet and put it on. The emblem on his back said Hells Angels Denmark. Yes, he knew they were troublemakers, but they were also his friends and had been for many years. They were the family he didn't have any longer. They took care of each other, even in jail where Peter had spent a few years. He knew he could count on his buddies anywhere at any time.

They just couldn't help him with this.

Peter knew he was old, and thought that he might be too old for riding a bike across Europe. But he didn't feel old. At the age of sixty-six, he felt strong, and his doctor had told him he was going to live for a long time. He had excellent vision and no diseases. He had made a lot of money over the years, along with his buddies, doing their business that he never told anyone about, laundering the money through Peter's carpentry company. Yes, Peter knew he had done many things he wasn't very proud of, but he had never hurt anyone by doing it, he kept telling himself.

Peter ran a hand across his silver hair and made a ponytail. He had showered one last time before he started packing. He took one last glance at the hallway mirror in his apartment, then lifted up the back-pack and swung it over his shoulder.

His doctor had told him he had many good years left to live; he wasn't going to waste them here. He wasn't going to let it all end on this forsaken island that had been his destiny and brought him so much sorrow.

Peter grabbed the door handle and swung the door open. Then he froze. On the other side, in the hallway, stood a tall, faceless figure dressed in a black suit and tie.

Peter gasped and stepped backwards, remembering the stories from his childhood they used to tell each other while playing in the woods at night. Stories about a tall man who lured little children to come to him before he killed them.

The tall, slender man stepped forward and, with a smooth movement, slit Peter's throat. In his dying moments, while bleeding to death on the tiles in his own apartment, Peter Larsen thought of his brothers. For the first time in many years, he dared to think of both of them.

39
***

JULY 1965

Ulrik Larsen hated working on his father's farm, but as time passed he was coming to terms with the fact that it was his destiny...it was his fate...his inheritance. Ulrik knew it was expected of him to take over from his father and, if anything, Ulrik was very good at living up to people's expectations. He figured out how to live with it. The work took up most of his waking hours, but every now and then he would take his bike and drive it the many kilometers to Nordby and visit the library. It could only happen on his monthly day off, but for Ulrik, it was worth the wait. He lived for those days. He lived and breathed for the last Saturday of every month.

He had even met a girl. At the library in downtown Nordby, he had met Jonna. She was the most beautiful girl he had ever laid eyes upon. And best of all, she liked to read as well. She helped out at the library and would always find five or six books for him that she thought he should read. They would spend the entire Saturday together, reading and laughing, and sometimes even going out for an ice cream on the harbor. Ulrik loved these Saturdays, when he was able to forget all about pigs and manure and the corn in the field.

He dreamt of marrying Jonna one day and having her come and

live on the farm with him. Being a city-girl, he knew it would require some adjustment for her, and he knew he would need to break it to her gently. She knew he lived and worked on a farm, and one Saturday he finally managed to invite her to come visit the farm and see where he lived and worked. He was terrified that she wasn't going to like it there, so before she arrived, he ran around cleaning up, even telling his mother and younger brother Per to dress nicely and be polite when speaking to her.

His mother giggled and put on a nice dress for his sake, while his youngest brother, Per, jumped the mud piles along with his friend Erling, who lived next door and always came over to play on the weekends.

Ulrik wasn't too pleased with them being around and asked his mother to keep them away from Jonna when she came. His mother didn't look too pleased when he mentioned it.

"It's Per's home too," she said. "He's having a friend over just like you, and they're entitled to be here just as much as you."

Ulrik growled and straightened his water-combed hair for the hundredth time, to make sure it stayed in place. He loved his mother, but she spoiled that kid way too much. Per could get away with anything, while Ulrik and Peter always had to earn their parent's praise by hard work. Ulrik envied both of his younger brothers so badly it hurt...to think they could both live the life they wanted. Ulrik would give anything to just be able to take off and go live in the city with Jonna and discuss books every day.

His mother held his head between her hands. She looked him in the eyes like she used to when he was younger.

"It'll be fine, Ulrik. Just wait and see. She'll love it here. If she loves you, she will. That's how I felt with your father."

Ulrik smiled wearily. He wasn't so sure she was right, but she still had a way of comforting him like no one else. Per and his friend Erling were screaming with joy outside the main house when Ulrik spotted Jonna on her bike riding across the gravel. Ulrik's heart stopped. Jonna's blond hair was lifted by the wind, her skirt fluttering beneath her. Ulrik smiled and watched her till she drove into the courtyard. Then he rushed out. He stood at the top of the stairs and waved as she parked her bike. Per and Erling whined with joy as one of the dogs joined their party in the mud pile. The sky was blue with a few clouds above them. It had been raining all morning, but finally seemed to be clearing up. It was perfect for the tour. The farm always looked best in sunshine.

"Hi, Ulrik," she yelled and waved back.

Her smile made his heart drop. Everything about her was just so... so perfect.

"Hi, Jonna," he said shyly, while Per and Erling made mocking sounds from their mud pile. Ulrik decided to ignore them. Jonna looked at him as he approached her, his head slightly bowed, his hand constantly making sure his hair stayed in place.

"So, this is where you live," she said with an enchanted light laughter. "It's beautiful, Ulrik. I love it. Look at those boys. Look at all the fun they have. And you have animals too?"

Ulrik dared to stand taller. He nodded. "Yes. Dogs, cats, and horses." He deliberately left out the pigs, since he thought they would be of no interest to a beautiful young girl like her. But he had misjudged her.

"Do you have any pigs?" she asked. "I simply adore pigs."

Ulrik smiled with a shy nod, and when Jonna grabbed his hand, he knew this was the best day of his life.

40

NOVEMBER 2014

It was hard for me to sleep that night. A thousand thoughts flickered through my mind. Mostly about this Facebook page. I couldn't stop wondering who would want to hurt me and Morten so badly. Who would go to this kind of extreme to hurt us?

I couldn't think of anyone. I tried to let it go and think about something else. Instead, I wondered about the killing of Ulrik Larsen and the mayor. I wasn't sure, but I had a feeling they had to be connected somehow and the faceless man, Slender Man, was the key. I had nothing to base my assumptions on, nothing but a gut feeling.

I grabbed my phone and looked at the clock. It was three o'clock. I had to get some sleep. I put my arm around a pillow and imagined it was Morten. I missed him like crazy and felt angry that we'd fought earlier. It was stupid. He was right to be frustrated, but to blame it all on me? That was taking it a little too far, I believed. On the other hand, maybe I should just let it go. He was desperate and needed someone to blame, and until we figured out who was behind this, I guess I was the best choice. Maybe I should just cut him some slack.

I closed my eyes and pictured Morten and me lying on a beach somewhere in Italy, holding hands. No kids, no dogs, just the two of us enjoying some time to ourselves. I liked the idea, and just before I finally dozed off, I decided to arrange a trip for the two of us. Maybe it should be Spain this time? Yes, I had a friend who lived in Malaga. We could go there and visit her. She had tried to get me to visit for ages. That was a wonderful idea. Maybe we could go just before Christmas? My parents could take care of Victor and Maya while we were away. We both needed some time off. I was going to talk to Morten about it in the morning. As long as I had no computer, I couldn't order the tickets myself anyway.

Boy, life was hard without the Internet. I didn't understand how people used to get by before we had it.

I fell asleep dreaming about sunshine and drinks in the sand, but woke up with a start. There was someone in my room. I gasped and turned my head. I stared into the face of Brutus. Then I screamed.

"Viiiictooor!!!"

Victor came in, looking at me indifferently. "What?" he asked.

"Your dog is staring at me in my sleep again. It freaks me out! Get him out of here!"

Victor shrugged, then grabbed Brutus' collar, but the dog didn't move. He kept staring at me with those white shining eyes that reflected the moonlight outside my window.

"Get him out of here, Victor. I can't sleep with him staring at me like that. It's creepy."

Victor pulled the collar again, but the dog still wouldn't move. It surprised me, since he usually obeyed Victor so well. But something was different. It was in his eyes. It was like he wanted to tell me something.

"Just get him out, Victor," I said again.

"He doesn't want to come," Victor said. "I guess he wants to sleep in here with you." Victor was about to leave, when I called him back.

"Don't leave that dog in here with me. You get him out of here, now, Victor. I'm not going to say it again. He drives me crazy with that staring."

Victor pulled the collar again. This time Brutus did react. He growled. He turned his head and growled at Victor. Victor pulled away, startled.

"That's it!" I said. "He's going back tomorrow! I've had it with that dog. I'm taking him back to the shelter tomorrow. Do you hear me, Brutus?"

He didn't look like he did. Instead, he opened his mouth and let out a loud and very deep bark. I gasped. The sound was very intimidating. Victor looked at me.

"I think he's trying to tell us something. We'd better listen."

41

NOVEMBER 2014

"What do you mean we better listen?" I asked. I looked at the clock on my phone again. It was getting really late. Actually, it was early in the morning now. I just really wanted to get some sleep.

The dog barked loudly again. There was something very profound about his bark. It sounded urgent, like he was insisting. It was strange, but I got the feeling that Victor was right. Brutus had something he wanted to tell us.

I looked at my son. "Then, you talk to him. Ask him what he wants."

Victor kneeled in front of Brutus. He bent his head and leaned in towards the dog till his forehead touched its snout. They sat like that for a little while before Victor finally rose to his feet. The dog then turned and walked out of the room.

"How did you do that?" I asked.

"He wants us to follow him."

"Do I have to?" I asked. The floor was so cold, and I really wanted to stay under the covers and catch up on my sleep before I had to get up.

"Come," Victor said.

I growled, found my slippers and a bathrobe, and followed Victor out of my room. As soon as I was in the hallway, the dog walked to the top of the stairs where it stopped.

"What is it? Is there someone down there?" I asked. The dog looked insistently at me.

My heart was suddenly pounding in my chest. What had the dog sensed? Had someone broken into our home? "Is there someone down there?" I asked again, like I was waiting for the dog to reply.

Carefully, I walked down the stairs, my heart racing in my chest. All day long, I had felt like I was being watched. Especially on my evening walk with the dogs, I had sensed there had been someone there with me in the darkness. Had this person followed me home? Had this person intruded into my house?

The dog and Victor stayed a few steps behind me. Brutus looked at the kitchen door in front of us.

"Is it in there? You want me to look in the kitchen?"

The dog kept staring. I grabbed the broom that stood next to the door to be able to defend myself if necessary, and then swung the door open. On the other side, I was met by a sight so horrifying I immediately threw up on the floor. I couldn't believe it. It was like a scene from some horror movie.

Oh, my God. Oh, dear God, no! Don't let this be true!

On the stove, in one of my grandmother's old pots, was Kenneth. The stove was on, and the water was boiling with poor Kenneth sitting lifelessly in it, his throat slit. My stomach turned again, as I tried to grasp the reality of the situation. I swayed briefly before I managed to pull myself together.

Who the hell could do such a cruel thing?

Thinking of my children, I wiped my mouth and shut the door, so Victor wouldn't see anything.

"Go upstairs and bring me my phone, will you?" I said, my voice shivering in desperation.

Luckily, Victor didn't notice anything. He simply shrugged with an "Okay" and stormed up the stairs.

I looked at Brutus.

"Thanks for the warning."

I walked back into the kitchen and turned off the stove. Holding back the urgent desire to throw up again, I took the pot to the sink and poured the contents out. I cried as I watched poor Kenneth fall into the sink with a thud. Sobbing, I picked up his lifeless body and put him in a small plastic bag. I found an empty shoebox in the closet and put Kenneth's tiny body inside of it and closed the lid. Seconds later, Maya came into the kitchen. She almost stepped in my vomit on the floor.

"What's going on here?"

Victor showed up behind her with my phone.

I looked at them both. I grabbed the phone while Maya waited for an answer.

"Sweetie," I said. "Sit down."

"What's going on?" Maya asked, with a slightly harsher voice. "You're scaring me, Mom."

"Sweetie. There has been...an accident. Kenneth...well, Kenneth is no longer with us."

"What do you mean he's no longer with us?" Maya looked startled.

I felt like crying myself, but held it back for Maya's sake. I put my hand on top of hers. "He's dead, sweetie. I just found him...he...he died."

Maya stared at me like she thought I was lying. I wasn't. Just withholding parts of the truth.

"We'll get you another dog, Maya, I promi..." But Maya didn't want to listen to me anymore. She rose to her feet with a moan. I could tell she was about to crack. I knew that face. So proud. Too proud to cry in front of her mother.

"Maya. Please..." I said. "We'll go to the shelter tomorrow. We'll find one that is just as cute."

Tears were welling up in her eyes. She tried to speak, but couldn't. She shook her head and bit her lip. "I loved that dog, Mom."

"I know you did. But these things happen. Dogs die. When you get a dog, you also get the sorrow that can come with it..."

Maya lifted her hands to signal she didn't want to hear anymore. "Why my dog? Why couldn't it have been Victor's ugly dog over there? Why mine?"

I had no answer. I had no words of comfort. I was still in shock myself.

42

NOVEMBER 2014

We stayed up all night eating my box of assorted chocolates that I had saved for a special occasion, and talking about Kenneth. When the sun came up, we walked into the yard and I dug a hole beneath one of the big pine trees. Maya put the shoebox in the hole and said a few nice words before we covered it all up.

I told her she could stay home from school if she wanted to, but she didn't. "I'll just miss him too much. The house is all empty without him, Mom."

I hadn't realized how much she had come to love him in just the short time we had the dog.

"Kenneth was special, Mom," she explained. "He was the only one around who didn't know me before I lost my memory. He understood me, Mom. We had something. He never demanded anything from me. He never looked at me angrily just because there was something I didn't remember. With him, I could be myself."

"Wow. I had no idea," I said, and grabbed her hand in mine. "Go get ready for school. I promise I'll take you to the shelter this afternoon."

Maya sobbed, then did as I told her.

"You mean to tell me someone went all *Fatal Attraction* on you and boiled your dog?" Sophia asked with wide eyes when she came over for coffee later. I had finally allowed myself to cry, since the kids had both left for school.

"Why Kenneth?" I asked sobbing. "Yes, he was annoying. Yes, he barked and ate my furniture, not to mention all of my shoes. Yes, I had sometimes thought about killing him myself, but come on? He was just a small dog. He never harmed anyone."

Sophia chuckled, but stopped herself. "I'm sorry," she said. "It's horrible. It really is, but...I'll shut up now."

I found a Kleenex and wiped my eyes. "I can't believe anyone would do such a horrible thing," I said. "Who on earth could hate me this much?"

"You think it's the same person as the one who made the Facebook page?" Sophia asked.

"I'm positive. This person is out to ruin my life. First, the Facebook page, which now has almost two thousand followers, by the way; I checked this morning on my iPad. Then, Morten's suspension...and, finally, this? Someone is out to really hurt my family. Who's next? Victor?"

Sophia looked at Brutus, who had somehow come into the kitchen without my knowledge, and apparently without opening any doors, as usual, since the door was still closed. How he did it remained a mystery to me. But everything about him was a mystery.

"You think anyone would want to hurt him?" Sophia asked, and nodded towards Brutus.

I shrugged. "He's not that easy to get close to, so I guess not." I exhaled heavily. "I'm just so freaking tired of sitting here waiting for the next disaster to hit."

"Then, don't," Sophia said and finished her coffee.

"What do you mean?"

"Look at you. You're a mess. It's so unlike you to just sit here and do nothing. Do something. Figure out who's behind this. There has to be some way."

"You're right. I have to find this person and make him pay. I'm so angry right now. I really want him to pay."

Sophia put her cup in the sink and grabbed her jacket from behind the chair. "Well, there you go. There isn't much else you can do now anyway, since you can't work on your book. Get busy getting back at this bastard." She looked at her watch. "I gotta go. I have a class in forty-five minutes."

"See you later. Do you and the kids want to come over for dinner tonight? My parents are coming too. Bring Jack as well. I really need to be surrounded by the people I love right now."

Sophia smiled. "Sure. That would be great."

She walked past Brutus, who stared at her with his white eyes as she passed him. Sophia shook her head. "Now, why didn't you bark when your little friend was cooked, huh?"

I looked up. "Oh, my gosh. You're right."

"Right about what?"

"Why didn't the damn dog bark when someone invaded our house and killed Kenneth? Why didn't it protect the house? I'll tell you why. Because it's someone we know. The dogs both knew this person."

43

NOVEMBER 2014

The revelation was both terrifying and intriguing. It was quite shocking because I had let this person inside of my home somehow. It was horrifying because I had let this person get close to my family and me, but at least I was now getting somewhere. At least it gave me something to work with. Now I knew that, not only was this person located here on the island, he also frequently visited my house, especially in the last week since we'd gotten the dogs. There weren't that many people who came into this house on a regular basis.

I started making a list.

I didn't get many names down before my phone rang. It was Morten. We hadn't spoken since our fight yesterday, and I was still a little angry with him.

"Hey. It's me," he said. "Listen, I'm sorry about yesterday. I was way off. Can you forgive me?"

I sniffled for my answer. I felt tears well up in my eyes. I tried to speak, but my voice cracked.

"What's wrong?" he asked. "Are you crying? It wasn't that bad of a fight, was it? Emma?"

"I'm sorry," I said. "It's just...there's a lot going on right now." I debated within myself whether I should tell him or not.

"What happened, Emma? I can tell something is wrong. Did something happen to one of the children?"

"No, no. They're both fine. But something did happen. Something awful."

"What, Emma? You're killing me here. Are you all alright?"

I decided to tell him. Even though I knew talking about it would only make me cry harder.

"It's Kenneth. He's dead." I cried as I spoke. "Someone broke into our house and killed him. They...they put him in a pot and..."

"Emma, this is serious," Morten said. "This is harassment. Breaking and entering. You need to talk to the police."

"I really don't want to," I said. "I'm not exactly popular with the police right now. I talked to my lawyer earlier this morning, and they're pressing charges against me for hacking. It could be serious, she says."

"I understand," Morten said. "But this can't go on. Someone is seriously harassing you, and it needs to stop."

I sniffled and picked up a Kleenex from the table. I wiped my tears away. "I'm just being silly," I said. "I mean, I wasn't even that fond of the dog. But Maya was, and I feel so bad for her."

"Plus, it's a lot to cope with...the fact that someone has been into your house. I really don't like this, Emma. You shouldn't be alone."

"I'm not alone. Brutus is here."

"That's good, but still. I worry about you. I'm on my way to Esbjerg now to talk to the chief of police, but I'll be back later and I'll come stay at your house."

"I invited my parents and Sophia and Jack over for dinner tonight," I said. I felt so thrilled Morten would be there as well. I was going to be with all the people I loved. It was just what the doctor ordered.

"Okay. Well, I'm at the police station in Esbjerg now. I'll call you later. Will you be okay?" Morten asked.

"Yes. Yes. I'll be fine. Good luck."

"Thanks."

We hung up and I wiped my nose on the Kleenex while looking at my list. So far, none of these people came off as anyone wanting to harm me, but I had thought that before, and it turned out that my own mailman was the one pulling the strings. I had to be careful with each and every person I let into my home, and wondered about the construction workers who had been here to finish the house. They had been in and out over the past several days, finishing some woodwork and painting the façade. It could easily be one of them.

I walked to the window and spotted them in the yard. The painters were on the ladder, chatting with the carpenters on the ground. They all seemed very happy. A radio played music.

I stared at them, as if I expected any one them to have blood on their hands or have the words dog-killer written on their faces, but was interrupted once again by my phone. This time it was an unknown number. I took it.

"Emma Frost."

"It's Michael."

I froze. "Michael?"

"I'm just calling to give you a heads up. I want to let you know that I'm taking Victor now."

"What do you mean?" I asked, my heart pounding.

"Well, you're about to go to jail, and your boyfriend is a sex offender. Unfortunately, Maya isn't mine, so I can't take her, but I'm taking Victor. I'm not letting him grow up with a criminal and a sex offender, that's for sure. My lawyer says it'll be easy as *one, two, three*."

44

NOVEMBER 2014

Lisa Rasmussen gurgled water to clear her throat. Then, she hummed a few notes and sang a scale to warm up her vocal chords. On the other side of the curtain waited the public in the main square of Nordby.

"This is it," her campaign manager Merethe said.

She annoyed Lisa slightly. Her jacket wasn't straight, and she had bad breath. The least she could do was to brush her teeth, considering all the money Lisa paid her.

"This is your big speech. This is when you get them to like you. Are you ready?" Merethe asked.

Her breath smelled like cheese. Lisa wrinkled her nose. On the table behind her stood the remains of her kale and cucumber smoothie. She wasn't going to finish it. Not right before speaking, in case any of the green stuff got stuck in her teeth. Lisa drank some more water and flushed her mouth.

"You've got this," Merethe said.

Was one of her teeth turning yellow?

"You can do it!"

Lisa had a tick in one of her eyes that wouldn't stop. Probably just nervousness. It had been a bad morning. She had woken up to the news that someone had decided to run against her in the election. An old woman named Jonna Frederiksen had decided she, all of a sudden, wanted to be mayor. She was so old that Lisa didn't understand why she was bothering, but to the local newspaper she had stated that it was on her bucket list; it was something she wanted to do before she died. Plus, she also believed she had many more years to live, and she could do wonderful things for the island. Especially since she had grown up there and knew every corner and every person. The last part annoyed Lisa immensely. That was the part she didn't have. This Jonna person was one of the locals. Lisa would never be, and she knew that people preferred their mayor to be one. It was one of their highest priorities, studies showed.

This speech was supposed to be her last speech, her solo appearance, since she was the only candidate, but now it was going to be a duel instead.

"I can do it," Lisa replied and repeated it while jumping up and down to warm up her muscles. "I can do this. I can do this."

The old lady suddenly turned up next to her backstage. Lisa recognized her from her picture in the paper. Jonna Frederiksen smiled. Lisa ignored her and kept repeating her mantra while jumping up and down.

"Good luck," Jonna said.

Lisa squinted her eyes, then looked at Merethe. "What does she mean by that?" she asked.

Merethe shrugged. "Focus on yourself and your own speech. You're going to win this, Lisa. You *are* the next mayor of Fanoe Island."

The words were comforting, even though Merethe's breath stunk like dead fish and seaweed. Lisa shook her head.

Focus. Focus. You're going to win this.

Lisa heard the announcer talking. He spoke of how important it was to remember to vote and repeated the date a few times before he finally said the words:

"Give it up for our two candidates. Jonna Frederiksen and Lisa Rasmussen!"

Lisa froze. Why had he said her name last? She looked at Merethe. Her ponytail wasn't straight. Lisa wanted to correct it.

"Go!" Merethe said.

Applause broke out, and Lisa realized she had missed the big entrance for which she had prepared so much. The old lady had already walked on stage, and now they were applauding her.

Crap!

Lisa rushed after her and onto the stage, putting on her famous election smile and waving at the maybe twenty people standing in front of the stage. They clapped unenthusiastically. Lisa kept smiling and waving while her opponent took her stand. Lisa found her place and adjusted the microphone. She cleared her throat and took in a deep breath.

"Let's give the first word to Jonna Frederiksen, who just announced her candidacy last night."

The audience applauded. Lisa growled as Jonna pulled the microphone closer and it made a howling noise. Lisa chuckled as she watched the audience cover their ears and make grimaces.

Amateur. Let her try if she likes. Let her have her dying wish. But mayor she will never become. That seat is mine. You hear me, old lady? It's mine!

45

NOVEMBER 2014

As if things weren't bad enough.

I put the phone down with a bad feeling in my stomach. I could hardly believe everything that was happening to me at once. It was simply surreal. It was like a really bad dream that I just couldn't slip out of.

I'm coming to get Victor.

The words kept lingering in my mind and I repeated them over and over again in my head. Michael had threatened this before, but for the first time, I was really afraid that he was going to succeed.

Once he heard about the breaking and entering, and the dead dog in my kitchen, on top of everything else, there was no way I would ever see my son again. I felt heartbroken and began looking for some candy I had hidden in the back of my cabinet when the phone rang again. My heart jumped, and at first I didn't want to pick it up in case it was him again, or just more bad news. I couldn't take anymore right now.

Still, I checked the display and saw Maya's name. I picked it up with a strongly beating heart. She wasn't allowed to turn her phone on during school. Something had to be wrong.

"What's up, honey? Aren't you in school?"

"Yes, I am," she said. "I'm in the restroom. I had to call you."

"What's going on?"

"I was in the computer lab this morning, checking my emails, since I can't do it at home anymore."

"Yeah, and so?" I looked out the window and kept an eye on the workers. They were on their coffee break, sitting under the big tree talking and drinking coffee out of their thermoses. It didn't really look like they were conspiring against me. But, then again, it only had to be one of them.

"I received this strange email. I got really scared, Mom."

I returned my focus to the conversation. "What kind of email?"

"This guy I know from school sent me an email telling me he just killed some guy, and that he did it because he loved me. Mom, it's really creepy."

"Are you sure it's not just some joke?" I asked.

"I...I don't know. But it's a very cruel joke, then. He talks about how this Slender Man has taught him everything and...and that he is one of his proxies, but he's doing it all for me, he says. I don't understand it, Mom. What is this?"

"I don't know, Maya. Does it say anything about who it is he claims to have killed?" I asked.

"Yes. It says I can go to this address and find the body, in case I don't believe him. It's like he thinks I think it's cool or something. But I don't, Mom. I really don't. I think it's so creepy."

"Of course you do, sweetie. Listen. Send me the address and I'll go check it out. It's probably nothing. Probably just some guy trying to be smart and get your attention. Send me the email. I'll read it on my phone and take a look at it. Don't worry about it anymore."

Maya sighed, relieved. "Thanks, Mom."

"No problem. Now get back to class before you get yourself in trouble."

I hung up and waited for the email to come through. It did almost immediately. I read the text and felt a shiver run down my spine.

Maya had been right. This was truly creepy. This boy clearly wasn't well. The question was whether he had really done what he claimed to. I had to find out. I was going grocery shopping anyway for tonight's dinner, so I might as well swing by this address and make sure everything was all right.

I filled Brutus' bowl with fresh water and food for a couple of hours, then rushed out to my car and drove off, forgetting the grocery list on the counter.

46

JULY 1965

They spent an enchanted day together at Ulrik's parents' farm. Jonna loved everything about the place and, little by little, Ulrik's many concerns for his future evaporated. Looking into her beautiful blue sparkling eyes and seeing all the excitement in them made him believe in his future for the first time in his life. Maybe it wasn't so bad, after all, that he had to take care of pigs for the rest of his life. Not if she would be by his side. Jonna put it all in a new perspective for him.

"Look at how happy the kids are here. All kids should grow up on a farm, if you ask me," she said, and pointed at Per and Erling, who were playing with the dogs, their clothes smeared in dried up mud. "Look!" she said again, and then let out a light laugh.

But Ulrik had only eyes for her. They had sat down at the table outside on the patio, where his mother was about to serve afternoon tea and buns. All day, she had been laughing like this and seeing things in a way Ulrik had never been able to. She had turned it all around and, suddenly, Ulrik was seeing it too. The pigs were adorable, cute even; the kids weren't noisy and annoying, they were happy and joyful; the mud was fun, the dogs for playing with, and the big trees surrounding the property were stunning. Oh, how Jonna had loved the trees. Perfect for lying beneath and reading a good book.

"And all this is going to be yours one day?" she had said, almost singing when he showed her the cornfields in the back.

For once, Ulrik had proudly answered, "Yes."

Ulrik's mother served them tea, and they sat in silence and drank and ate while the kids continued their playing. Ulrik saw how his mother looked at Jonna, and knew that she liked her. She had even brought out the nice China. The dishes she had inherited from Ulrik's great-grandmother.

"It's such a wonderful place you have here, Mrs. Larsen," she said. "You must all be very happy."

Ulrik's mother smiled and poured Jonna another cup of tea. Jonna put sugar in it and stirred.

"We are very happy here," Ulrik's mother said, just as Ulrik's dad joined them.

He grunted angrily as he sat down and his wife poured him tea. He slurped and ate the bun that his wife had buttered for him. His hands were dirty, and he smelled like pig. Ulrik looked at Jonna, fearing that she would be scared off. But she didn't seem to be. She smiled at Ulrik's dad.

"I was just telling your wife what a beautiful farm you have, Mr. Larsen," she said joyfully. "It must be such a joy to be able to work outside like this every day."

Ulrik's dad stopped chewing, then nodded. "Sure is," he said. "Tell that to this kid here. He seems to think the only thing in the world worth doing is burying his nose in a book." Ulrik's dad finished his sentence with a grunt, then continued to chew his bun. "Let me have another one," he said to his wife.

She buttered one for him. "Could I get you to take down Peter's dinner to old Hansen's after you're done eating?" his mother then asked. "He's staying till it gets dark tonight."

Ulrik sighed. "But that's gonna take the rest of the afternoon.

Jonna and I were planning on going to the library downtown before I escort her home."

Ulrik's dad grunted again. "You do as your mother tells you, son. Take the two bandits with you as well. Your mother can't keep an eye on them and cook dinner at the same time."

"But..."

"Do as your mother tells you," his dad repeated, and gave him a look telling him there would be no arguing. Ulrik knew to stop. It was no use arguing with his father, even if he tried. Ulrik looked at Jonna, who put her hand on top of his. "We'd be glad to be of help," she said. "It's no problem."

47

NOVEMBER 2014

The address led me to an apartment in downtown Nordby. It was located on the main street, looking out at the square. A very nice location, I thought. The street was closed to cars, so I parked further down the road and walked the rest of the way. I had to cross the square to get to the apartment. Something was going on in the center of it. A stage had been set up, and people had gathered to listen. It was the candidate's last debate. I had read about it in the newspaper that had been my main source of information ever since I had lost my computer. Well, that and Sophia.

Apparently, there was a last minute candidate for the election, challenging Lisa Rasmussen. To be frank, I really wanted to hear what she had to say; I really wanted her to be better than Lisa, whom I thought was very odd. But that wasn't why I was there. I could read all about it in the morning paper, so I hurried past and found the right building. I looked at my phone and checked that I had the right address. I did. I buzzed a couple of buttons, and told some old lady that I was the paperboy. Strangely enough, she bought it.

I walked up the stairs till I reached the third floor. There were two apartments there, but according to the email, it was the one to the right. I looked at the door, and the name on the outside.

PETER LARSEN

The name made me wonder. It was, after all, less than a few days ago that another Larsen had been brutally murdered in his home. It was, of course, a fairly common name in this country, but still? Helle Larsen's second son had been a Peter.

My heart beat fast as I rang the doorbell. There was no answer. I knocked, still nothing. I opened the letterbox in the door.

"Hello? Peter Larsen? Are you home?"

There was no answer, but something else was there. Flies. A ton of them. They swarmed around my face. I spat and pulled my head back. Then I grabbed the handle and pulled it. The door was open. This wasn't a good sign. People didn't leave their homes unlocked. At least not anymore. I had been told that there used to be a time when people on this island would never lock a door.

I saw him as soon as I opened the door. Well I saw someone sitting in a chair with his back turned at me. A long track of blood across the carpet in the hallway told me something bad had happened here. There was also a smell.

"Hello?"

I walked closer to the figure in the chair in the living room with the long silver ponytail. I felt anxious. Should I call Morten and ask him to come before I proceeded? Should I have just sent the email to the police, instead of coming here all on my own? Would they believe me with everything else that was going on?

I swiped away the many flies surrounding me and walked cautiously towards him. His head was bent forward. He was tied to the chair with a thick rope.

"Hello? Peter Larsen?"

I approached the man with an eerie feeling inside.

He's not moving. He's not answering. Something is wrong here. Something is very wrong. Please, let him be asleep. Please, let him just be asleep.

I walked around the man in the chair, expecting the worst, but nothing I could have imagined could ever have prepared me for this.

Oh, the horror. I didn't even know this was possible?

The man's throat had been cut horizontally with a sharp object, and his tongue was pulled out through the open wound, making it look like a necktie.

I gagged, then turned around and threw up for the second time this day.

48

NOVEMBER 2014

"Let me start off by telling you all a little story," Jonna Frederiksen began.

Lisa rolled her eyes with a smirk.

Now isn't that sweet? The old lady wants to tell stories. Well, go ahead, granny. Bore them to death.

"The other day I was on my way home from SuperBrugsen. I had just bought some milk and a few other things."

Come on! Please! Who cares what you bought in the supermarket. This is an election, for crying out loud.

But, much to her surprise, the audience seemed to be interested in her story. Lisa looked at their faces and realized most of them were also old. They could relate to what she was saying, couldn't they?

Damn!

In the crowd, Lisa spotted a reporter from the local paper. She knew how important it was to get him to write about her key issues. Merethe had told her how important he was, and now he was looking all interested at the old lady.

"When I had put my purse in the basket on my bike, a car drove up next to me and a person approached me. She said she needed

directions, but I had never heard of the place before, and soon I realized that it was a scam."

Lisa widened her eyes. What was this? Did she have something interesting to say? Did she have a cause?

"As it turns out, the guy in the car tried to steal my purse from my basket, but I grabbed him by the ear and made him give it back. Then, I sent them both off and told them to never show their faces here on the island again. I can tell you, they were suddenly in a hurry," she said, and laughed.

Lisa was paralyzed. The crowd laughed too, and now they were applauding her. The journalist was writing on his pad and taking pictures of her. What was this? He was supposed to take pictures of Lisa. She was the winner here!

"But, jokes aside," Jonna Frederiksen continued. "To me, this was a turning point. I grew up on this island. I remember a time when we didn't have to lock our doors. A time when there was no crime here, and everyone could walk safely at night. The last two years, we've had people being brutally killed, we've had people disappearing and never being found, and our own mayor for numerous years was killed in what is believed to be an arson-fire. We're losing the tourists. Stories about them possibly getting their valuables and wallets stolen by criminal Eastern European gangs are spreading widely and scaring them away. Criminals are coming here to exploit the fact that we are not used to crime; we are not properly protected. I say we take back charge of things. I say we bring back security."

Oh, no she didn't! She pulled the local-card! It's not fair. I can never be a local. I can never tell stories about how it used to be. Did she mention the Eastern Europeans? That was my key-issue. That was supposed to be my cause, the one I got elected on! What the hell is this bitch trying to do?

Desperately, Lisa looked at Merethe, who was standing behind the curtain. She shrugged when Lisa signaled her what was going on? More people had started to gather, attracted by the story, and faces were listening to the old woman with great interest. Some were

nodding in recognition of the problems she pointed out, others were looking at the person next to them and agreeing.

You need to do something, Lisa. She's got them! They like her! They love her, for crying out loud! You have to do something!

"So, that is why if you elect me, dear fellow islanders, I will fight for the local police to be strengthened, and not cut back as they are trying to now. I will fight to get the criminals off this island. We've never had crime like this here before, and we never will again."

Do something now! You need to say something, something that tops whatever she said.

Lisa leaned forward, grabbed the microphone and yelled. "I couldn't agree more. Hey, my name is Lisa Rasmussen, but most of you already know that, since you've probably seen my picture on posters, but I completely agree with Jonna Frederiksen here. The Eastern Europeans pose bigger and bigger problem for our tourists. We have all seen how it's going down; we have all felt it in our businesses. But they are not the only problem we're facing here on the island. That's why, if you elect me, I'll make sure to fight so that not only will the Eastern Europeans be unable to come here and do their crime, but also the Asians. Yes, you heard me right. Asians pose huge problems today. Just the other day, I had a very unpleasant encounter with one. They come here with their unsanitary ways and bring all these diseases with them. They bring them to our food in the supermarket; they sneeze in public places. They have SARS, MERS, and the flu. Yes, that's what they bring here...rats and bird flu. And they bring it all to the supermarket!"

Lisa looked at the many estranged faces in the crowd, and realized she might have lost them a little. Yet, she continued.

"And Ebola," she said, trying desperately to find a common ground, something they could all agree on. "We need to fight Ebola."

The faces didn't look any less alienated. Lucky for her, the entire debate was interrupted when someone burst out of one of the buildings facing the square, yelling and screaming in terror.

49

NOVEMBER 2014

"**H**ELP!"

I was screaming as I ran out of the building. The terror of what I had seen had overwhelmed me, and I couldn't stop yelling.

"Call the police. There's been a murder!"

Someone ran to me and grabbed my arm. It was the reporter from *Fanoe Times*, Hans Lejbach. He had his camera around his neck and a notepad in his other hand.

"Emma Frost?" he said, startled. "What's going on?"

"A man...in a chair...dead. Call the police!" I stuttered.

"Where?"

"In that building," I said, panting desperately, suppressing my desire to scream again. The images of the man still flickered before my eyes; my heart raced in my chest. I pointed. "Third floor to the right."

Hans Lejbach reached into his pocket and found his phone. He walked away while talking to the police. Others came running, and soon I was surrounded. I felt dizzy and fell to my knees.

"What happened?" I heard someone say.

"It's Emma Frost," another whispered.

"Oh," someone else replied.

Turmoil broke out. People were whispering and murmuring about me. I tried to block them out, while catching my breath. At first, I wanted to explain. I wanted to tell them why I had hacked, that I had never used it for bad things, that it had helped solve murder cases and that my boyfriend was innocent, that he certainly wasn't a pervert, but then I realized I didn't owe them any explanations. It didn't matter what they thought. Besides, they wouldn't believe me anyway. It was no use.

I was still bent over on my knees, trying to calm down, when a hand reached out to me. I lifted my head and spotted Jonna Frederiksen, the new candidate. She smiled. I put my hand in hers, and she helped me up.

"Emma Frost?" she said.

I nodded.

"I've read all of your books and loved each and every one of them."

I looked at the old lady with the warm hands. "Thanks," I said, quite surprised by this sudden gesture. The people surrounding us went quiet. I got the feeling they had great respect for the old lady.

"No problem. Us islanders must help one another," she said.

The police came, and I gave my testimony to Allan. I told him what had happened, how I had known from the email, how I had gone out there to see if it was true, and found him. Allan nodded and wrote everything down on his pad. When he was done, he looked up at me.

"Thanks, Emma. By the way, I'm sorry for all the trouble lately. How's Morten holding up? We miss him at the station."

"He's at a meeting with the chief in Esbjerg right now. But he's not good. He's frustrated. It was a set-up."

Allan nodded. "I know. None of us believe he would ever do such a thing. I just hope he comes back soon."

"So, what do you think about this?" I asked, and looked up at the building.

Allan scratched his head. "It's ugly. The way he was killed, I mean. It's what they call a Columbian Necktie. I've read about it, but never actually seen it. Quite nasty."

"Was he related to Ulrik Larsen, who died the other day?" I asked.

"Brother. Ulrik was the oldest," Allan said.

"So, I guess it's fair to say that the two killings were related, huh?"

"Probably not a bad assumption."

"And the mayor?"

"What's that?" Allan asked.

"The murder of the mayor. Could that be related?" I asked.

"We're investigating them separately. I can't see any link between them. Plus, the mayor and Ulrik didn't know each other, according to the mayor's wife. Well, I'd better..." Allan signaled that he had to get back to work. I grabbed his arm and held him back.

"So, are you arresting this kid, this Tommy Malthesen, who sent the email to my daughter?" I asked.

"We'll take him in right after we're done here. Now, say hi to Morten from me, will you? And stay out of trouble."

50

JULY 1965

They rode their bikes to old Hansen's farm. Erling and Per stayed a few meters behind them on the road, so Ulrik and Jonna could talk. They discussed the murder of Malcolm X, and Jonna told him that she heard there was a book coming up this fall, an autobiography that they both agreed they simply had to read.

Ulrik sighed and looked at Jonna.

"What?" she said shyly.

"I've never met anyone who wanted to discuss Malcolm X before. I've never met anyone as interesting to talk to as you are. I thought I was the only one with a passion for books."

Jonna blushed. It didn't make her any less beautiful. On the contrary. Even blushing looked good on her. Ulrik watched her and reached out his hand to grab hers while they biked down the road and turned into the gravel that marked the beginning of old Hansen's property.

"So, what does your brother do for this man?" Jonna asked.

"Handiwork, I guess. The old man is all alone, and has no sons. So, he pays Peter to fix stuff around the farm. Peter's been saving his money. He wants to travel when he's done with high school. I guess I envy him a little. I would love to see the world. It's silly, but I once had a dream of visiting libraries all over the world."

"That's not silly," Jonna said. "I kind of like that idea."

Ulrik chuckled. "Yeah it would be nice. But having to take care of my father's farm takes all of my time. I'm not sure there will be much time for traveling in my future."

Jonna shrugged. "You never know how life will turn out."

"I guess not."

Ulrik liked that. Jonna was so right. You really never knew what life would turn out like, did you? Up until a few months ago, he had never thought he would meet a girl like her. He never thought he would be able to discuss important things with anyone again, since he stopped going to school. He thought the rest of his life would be all about pigs and corn. But along she came, and everything was changed. Maybe there would be traveling in his future, after all. Maybe he was going to visit libraries and museums all over the world. Maybe some day...

They drove their bikes into the courtyard. It was very quiet at the farm. The dogs were sleeping by the stairs.

"Where is he?" Jonna asked.

Per and Erling threw their bikes in the grass and started fighting and laughing. Ulrik shook his head. He wondered what was ever going to become of his baby brother. He was so wild. So out of control. Well, it was entirely their mother's fault, wasn't it? She spoiled him so much. She thought he could never do anything wrong.

"He might be in the barn," Ulrik said, and pointed. He hoped he was right. He wanted so badly to get this over with, to deliver the bag with food, then get back and drop off the two boys, so he could once again be alone with Jonna. He still had a bike ride to town, and maybe they might catch an hour at the library before she had to be home. If he hurried up, they could just make it.

"Don't go anywhere, boys," he said to Per and Erling. "Stay close. We're leaving as soon as I deliver this to Peter." He grabbed the sack his mom had packed with rye bread sandwiches, and started walking towards the barn. Jonna walked next to him and grabbed his hand in hers.

"Peter?" Ulrik called. "Peter?"

Ulrik had spotted his bike over by the main building, so his younger brother was still there. It was all about finding out where he could be, and preferably in a hurry.

"Let's try the barn first," he said, still looking around to see if he might spot him somewhere else.

Ulrik grabbed the handle on the big gate to the barn and pulled it aside. But the barn was empty except for an old tractor and a lot of bales of straw.

"Peter?"

"Maybe he's somewhere else," Jonna said. "Maybe we should go to the main house and ask Mr. Hansen?"

Ulrik had hoped to be able to make the delivery without having to face the old man. He had never liked him much. He gave him the creeps.

"Sure," he said, thinking it was by far the smartest move, since old Hansen would know what he had asked Peter to do for him. "Come on, boys. We'll knock on the door to the main house. Follow me."

Ulrik walked up the stairs and stopped in front of the door. Two dogs were sleeping heavily outside. One of them opened his eyes and took one glance at Ulrik, then went back to sleep. Ulrik knocked. There was no answer. He knocked again. "Mr. Hansen? It's Ulrik Larsen!"

Ulrik growled in irritation. "Hansen is old," he said. "Probably can't hear us."

The door was ajar and opened when he tried to knock again. Ulrik stepped inside. Jonna paused.

"You think it's okay to just go in?" Jonna asked.

"Sure. I've been here a million times. The old man probably can't hear us, or maybe he's fallen asleep. I can give him the sack, and then he can give it to Peter. He might be working all the way down on the other end of the paddocks. He might be repairing the fence or something. We could end up spending the rest of the afternoon looking for him. This way is much easier."

"Alright," Jonna said, and they all followed Ulrik inside the house. It smelled like old wet dog inside. Ulrik looked at Jonna, who held her nose.

"Mr. Hansen?" he yelled. "It's Ulrik Larsen. I brought dinner for Peter."

"Maybe we should just put it in the kitchen, if he's not here" Jonna whispered.

Ulrik thought it was an excellent idea. Hopefully, they would find it. If they didn't, then his brother would survive. Ulrik loved his brother, but he wasn't spending all day on this. Not when he could spend time with Jonna.

"I thought I heard something," Jonna said, all of a sudden.

Ulrik heard it too. "Must be the old man."

"It sounds like it came from down the hallway."

Ulrik looked at Jonna. "I'll just leave the food in the kitchen," he said.

Jonna gave him a look. "You can't do that. If no one knows it's there, then he'll never get it. Your brother will starve. You have to at least tell the old man, so he can tell Peter. It's the least you can do."

Ulrik sighed. He knew she was right. But he really didn't want to have to walk into one of the rooms and talk to the old man. Jonna pushed him gently. "Go on. The sounds are coming from behind that door over there."

"Okay," he said, and started walking. Jonna and the boys were right behind him. Per and Erling were very quiet for once. Probably scared to death of the old house, Ulrik thought to himself. The sounds became louder and louder as they approached the door, and Ulrik wondered for just a second what was going on behind that door. Still, he grabbed the handle and pulled the door wide open, so wide that all of them saw what was on the other side of it. On the bed, tied down with a leather belt, lay his brother. His beautiful innocent brother strapped down, naked, and on top of him was the old man...forcing himself on him.

Ulrik gasped. Jonna let out a small shriek.

"What the hell is going on here?" Ulrik yelled. As he did, his eyes met Peter's, and he realized Peter was crying.

"Help me," he wheezed, barely able to breathe underneath the heavy weight of the old man.

In that second, Ulrik blacked out. Later on, when trying to recall what happened, he would remember yelling something, then turning around and grabbing old Hansen's rifle that was leaned against the wall behind the door. He would remember yelling for the old pervert to get the hell off his brother, while pointing the rifle at him. He would remember the old wrinkled body moving, the loose skin dangling, and the face pleading and telling him he couldn't help himself, telling him to have mercy on an old man. He would remember all that, including the look in the old man's eyes as he fell to his knees and Ulrik yelled and screamed at him till everything exploded inside of him. He would remember that. But he wouldn't remember firing the rifle. He wouldn't remember Jonna screaming. He wouldn't remember the blood spurting or the brain mass sprayed on the wall behind the old man as his face exploded. No, Ulrik wouldn't remember the details of this event for many years afterwards, but his brothers and friends would. And they would never ever forget.

51

NOVEMBER 2014

I was quite shaken, still, when I returned to my house. The images of the old man sitting in his chair with his tongue pulled out through his neck, wouldn't leave me. I poured myself a whiskey and sat down in the living room. Brutus was staring at me from the corner. I sighed and looked at him.

"Is that all you do, huh?"

I drank from my glass, then grabbed my iPad from the coffee table and googled Columbian Necktie. Apparently, it was first used during the outbreak of La Violencia, the Colombian civil war from 1948 till 1958. It was intended as a method of psychological warfare, meant to scare and terrorize. Today, it was used by drug kingpins to intimidate others.

I took another sip of my whiskey, wondering how this could have anything to do with what was going on here on our little island.

I never finished the thought before Morten walked in the door. I had left a message on his voicemail about what had happened. I was pretty out of it at the time, so I had probably scared the crap out of him.

"Emma?" he yelled.

"In the living room!" I yelled back.

He stormed inside. "Are you alright?"

I tilted my head from side to side, then lifted my glass. "This helps a little."

He relaxed a little when he saw my smile. He took off his jacket and put it on a chair, then sat down next to me on the couch. "That sounded like a bad scare. Did you say his tongue was pulled out of the wound?"

"A true Columbian Necktie, yes."

He wrinkled his forehead. "That sounds nasty."

"It was." I finished my drink and could feel the effect. Helped calm me down. "A kid, some teenager admitted to having done it in a letter to Maya. It's all a mess."

"You want me to get you another one?" he asked.

I shook my head. "No. The kids are coming home in a little while, and I've invited almost everyone we know over for dinner, so I have to cook all afternoon. I can't be drunk. I don't have the time."

Morten chuckled. I put my head on his shoulder. "So, how was your meeting?"

Morten exhaled.

"That bad, huh?" I said. "Maybe I should pour you a drink?"

"Nah. I'll get some red wine later tonight. That should be enough."

I lit up. "You're staying the night?"

"Oh, yeah. Jytte is at a friend's house anyway."

"A party?"

Morten shrugged. "I hope not."

"At that age, you never know," I said, thinking of how much I used to party when I was in high school. I thought of Maya and wondered when it would start for her. Usually, Danish kids started drinking at the age of thirteen or fourteen, but I didn't think she had started yet. I was happy she hadn't, since I thought it was way too early, but I hoped that she still had a good social life, and that she wasn't missing out. Nah, it would come eventually. I wasn't really looking forward to having to pick her up at someone's house all wasted, so I was in no hurry.

"So what did the chief of police say?" I asked.

"There was an entire committee there. I told them my story. Told them how we're being harassed. I'm still suspended, but they told me they had heard my story and they'd wait for the investigation to be done before they made their final decision. I did what I could, now it's no longer in my hands. They're not going to find any more bad things on my computer, so now it's up to them whether they'll give me the benefit of the doubt."

I put my arm around his neck and hugged him from behind. "I'm sure you'll get your job back soon."

"I hope so. I miss it."

I was trying to think of something truly comforting to say, when the kids suddenly came home. I served them afternoon tea with toasted bread and jam.

"When can we go look for a new dog?" Maya asked.

"Done," Victor exclaimed, then jumped out of his chair and sprang for the yard. "Don't forget your jacket!" I yelled after him.

"So, when can I?" Maya repeated.

I exhaled and sipped my tea. I really wasn't in the mood to have to go down to that shelter once again and pick out a dog. "Dr. Sonnichsen will be here any moment," I said. "So, it'll have to wait."

"So, maybe after we're done?" Maya said.

"I..." Maya's eyes were pleading. I felt so bad for her. She had really loved Kenneth. "I've invited Sophia and the kids and grandma and grandpa over for dinner. I have a ton of work..."

Maya jumped out of her chair and stomped her feet. "I knew it! I knew you wouldn't keep your promise. It's so UNFAIR!" she yelled and stormed out the door. I heard her angry steps on the stairs and then her door slam hard. Music was soon thumping.

Morten chuckled. "Glad to see that she's getting better," he said.

I grabbed another piece of toast and put jam on it. The doorbell rang, and I went to open it. It was Dr. Sonnichsen. She was holding an umbrella over her head. The rain was pouring heavily outside.

"Good afternoon," she chirped, as she closed the umbrella.

"Maya's upstairs," I said. "She's a little upset. We...well, Kenneth died last night. She'll tell you the rest."

"Naturally," Dr. Sonnichsen said. She seemed to be completely unmoved by the fact that the dog had died.

"I'll talk to her," she simply said.

"Thanks. You really are a lifesaver. I wouldn't know what to do without you." I closed the door behind her and let her walk inside. Brutus was sitting at the bottom of the stairs, blocking her way.

"Hi, Brutus," Dr. Sonnichsen said, and approached him.

The dog stared at her with its white piercing eyes. Then he did something I had never seen him do. He got up, raised the hair on his back, and growled at the doctor.

"Brutus!" I said. I looked at the doctor. She seemed perplexed. "I'm sorry. He doesn't usually do this. Brutus, move away from the stairs!"

Brutus didn't move an inch. The doctor whimpered and pulled back.

"I'm sorry. He usually never growls," I said.

"Well, he is a pit bull, isn't he? They're known to be the nicest of dogs, then suddenly one day, turn on their owner for no apparent reason."

I looked at the doctor, who tried to squeeze by the dog. I had never heard that before. I grabbed Brutus' collar and pulled him back. He turned and snarled at me.

"Brutus!" I said, while Dr. Sonnichsen disappeared up the stairs. I couldn't believe he had growled at me. To be honest, he was scaring me more than ever. Especially after what the doctor had said. I wondered if it was safe to have him in the house, this close to my children.

Victor came in through the patio door. "Brutus!"

The dog immediately reacted. It wagged its tail and walked towards him like a completely different dog.

"Brutus. Where did you go? We were in the middle of a game. Come."

I watched as the dog walked off with my son. Morten put his arm around me.

"Can you believe that?" I asked. "I tell you, that dog freaks me out. I can't have him growling at people coming to my house. I'm afraid he might attack someone some day."

Morten chuckled. "I'm sure it'll be fine. Now, what were you planning on making for dinner?"

"Dinner! I completely forgot. I'm having company in just three hours, and I have no idea what to make yet."

52

NOVEMBER 2014

"Hi, Maya, how are you today?"

The numerologist walked in the door to Maya's room and found her on the bed. She was crying. Music was pounding from the speakers on the floor. The numerologist turned the music down.

"Oh my, Maya. Are you alright?" She sat on the bed and looked at the girl. Maya hid her head in her pillow. "It's okay, sweetheart. You can tell me what's wrong. I won't tell anyone."

Maya said something into the pillow, but nothing but muffled sounds came out.

"I heard something bad happened to Kenneth?" the numerologist said. "I'm so sorry to hear that he was killed. I can't believe anyone could do such a cruel thing to your poor dog."

Maya moved the pillow. "Killed?"

The numerologist smiled. "Yes."

Maya looked like she didn't believe her. The numerologist wondered if she had said too much. Apparently, the girl didn't know.

"Well, let's not talk about that anymore," the numerologist said. "I understand you being upset. It is hard to lose your dog."

Maya sat up. "What do you mean he was killed?"

The numerologist reached into her bag and pulled out a book. "Let's not talk anymore. Today, I thought we should look into…"

"You mean to tell me someone killed my dog?" Maya continued. She was not letting this go.

"Well yes, or…I don't know, Maya."

"Was that why she didn't want me to see him before we buried him? What happened to him?"

"I don't know, Maya. Maybe you should ask your mother about that. I don't even know if he was killed or maybe he died of natural causes. Maybe he ate something."

Maya shook her head. "No. No. You said you couldn't believe anyone would do something that cruel. That's what you just said. You know what happened, don't you? Spit it out. I want to know."

The numerologist felt sweat break out on her forehead. She closed her book and looked at Maya. "Now, Maya. I'm not going to say this more than once…"

The numerologist stopped when the doorbell rang downstairs and voices suddenly filled the house. They weren't ordinary voices. They were angry voices, people yelling downstairs.

"What on earth is going on?" the numerologist asked. Maya walked to the door and opened it. "I don't know. But one of the voices sounds like it belongs to my dad."

She walked into the hallway and the numerologist followed. They stood on top of the stairs and listened to the angry yelling. Maya's dad was the one yelling the loudest.

"I am taking him with me now. He's not going to spend one more day in the company of that sex offender, that…that pervert. I can't believe you'd expose my son to that. I can't believe you, Emma! Where is he?"

Maya's father stepped forward in a threatening motion.

"You're not taking him, Michael," Emma yelled back. "Nothing has been settled yet. As far as I know, we still have joint custody over him. And he's staying here until you have a court's order that states otherwise. He's my son, Michael."

"Goddammit, Emma. He's my son too."

The numerologist stared at the scene with a huge smile she couldn't restrain. This was excellent. By far, better than anything she had hoped for.

"I'm going to get him now, Emma. You can't stop me. You can't keep me from him. I'm his father, for crying out loud. I want him. And I'm taking him now."

Michael stepped forward, when Emma's boyfriend Morten stepped out in front of him. "You're not going anywhere. This is private property, and you're trespassing right now. You're not welcome here."

Michael looked at Morten, then lifted his clenched fist in the air and smacked him. Morten fell backwards. Emma Frost screamed.

"You bastard!"

The numerologist felt like clapping and dancing. This was so much FUN!

Morten was back on his feet now and took a swing at Michael. He hit him on the jaw and Michael fell backwards. Michael then stormed forward and tumbled Morten to the ground. Morten kicked and managed to get Michael off him. Michael grabbed him by the collar and lifted him up, then swung his fist and hit him twice in the face. Emma screamed. The numerologist laughed. Emma grabbed a lamp from the small table, swung it, and smashed it on Michael's head. He fell backwards to the ground with a loud yell. Emma stood bent over him, still with the remains of the lamp in her hand. She looked like she would hit him with it again, but instead, she yelled.

"Get the hell out of here, you bastard."

Michael got up to his feet. Humping and whining, he got out of the front door. Morten ran after him.

"If I ever see you again, I swear, I'm gonna kill you!" he yelled.

The numerologist stayed on the stairs with a big smile on her face. *Oh, will you now?*

53

NOVEMBER 2014

"I'm not going to lie to you. It doesn't look good."

Merethe looked at Lisa over her glasses. She was still standing in the doorway of Lisa's house. It was early morning. Lisa hadn't gotten the kids out of the house yet, and Christian was upstairs in the shower. Usually, Lisa wouldn't have let anyone come over this early, but Merethe had insisted on the phone that it was important. She had a crumb on her chin. Had she gained weight since yesterday? Lisa believed she had. She looked chubby; her leggings were tight on her. People that chubby shouldn't be wearing leggings at all, in Lisa's opinion.

"May I come in?"

Lisa moved out of her way, and Merethe walked in. She took off her coat and put it on a chair. Lisa scoffed, then found a hanger and put the coat in the closet where it belonged. Merethe walked into the living room, still wearing her shoes. It made Lisa's skin crawl. She hated when people didn't take off their shoes in her home. Her white carpets stained so easily.

"Mom, where is my backpack?" Amalie came out from the kitchen and looked at her mother. It was amazing how helpless children could be, even at the age of fifteen, Lisa thought, and pointed at the back-pack leaned neatly up against the wall in the hallway, all packed and ready for her daughter to simply pick it up and run out the door. Just like it always was. How hard was it to know after all these years?

"Thanks," Amalie said, then sprang for the door.

Not even a proper goodbye.

"Let's do this in the kitchen," Lisa said, looking at Merethe's dirty shoes that were already planted solidly on her white carpet. Lisa took in a deep breath, trying hard to calm herself down. In the kitchen, Merethe took out an iPad and tapped on it. Lisa wondered if Christian would be able to drop off Jacob in time for his classes to start. Margrethe was running around the kitchen with a doll in her arms. She approached Merethe with a small shriek, and gave her leg a hug. Lisa picked her up and put her on her lap.

"These are today's articles," Merethe said, and handed Lisa the iPad so she could see. She read the headline of the local paper.

IS LISA RASMUSSEN A RACIST?

"It's basically all the same," she said. "Even the local bloggers are writing about it. They all think your remarks about Asians were very racist. It's not good. Your numbers are down. If they continue like this, you'll end up losing the election on Tuesday."

Lisa scrolled the article frantically, while Margrethe tried to reach out for it. Lisa felt like her blood was boiling. What was this? How could they be this stupid? Hadn't she just said what everyone else was thinking?

"I...I don't understand," she said.

"Lisa. You can't make racist remarks against a certain group of people," Merethe explained. "Remarks like those you made yesterday will make people turn their backs on you. It can break a political career in an instant. You have to be more careful. Now, the way I see it, we still have many good things to work on, but we need serious damage control. We need to turn the people's mood. We need to get the voters back somehow. What we need is something big. Something that brings people's sympathy back towards you."

Lisa stared at the article. Christian came into the kitchen. Margrethe saw her father and reached out for him. He grabbed her in his arms.

"Well, we're off," he said. "You girls have a good time."

Lisa hardly noticed him. She waved, distracted, while still looking at the article. "Hmmm, bye, sweetie."

The door slammed and Lisa finally looked up at Merethe. "So, how do we do that?" she asked. "How do we bring the sympathy back?"

Merethe shrugged. "I have no idea. I thought you might be able to come up with something good?"

Lisa stared at her campaign manager.

Is that dirt underneath her nails?

Who did she thinks she was anyway? She was the one Lisa was paying a lot of money to make sure she won this election. She was supposed to come up with the ideas here.

Yes, it's definitely dirt. Doesn't she ever wash her hands? Think of all the diseases and germs that could be under her nails. She brings that into my house?

"Well, I guess we'll have to put our heads together and come up with something, won't we?" Merethe said, and finally removed the crumb with her dirty nails when she scratched herself on the chin. The crumb fell onto the kitchen table, and Lisa stared at it, wondering if Merethe would pick the germ filled dirty crumb up herself, or if she expected Lisa to do it.

54

NOVEMBER 2014

"DINNER WAS GREAT YESTERDAY."

Morten leaned over and kissed me gently. I smiled and held his face between my hands.

"Yes it was," I said. "It was so nice just to hang out with everybody that I love."

"Even though Sophia's kids were quite noisy at the table," Morten said.

"Well, she's got a lot on her plate, having six children. You need to cut her some slack. I don't know how I would survive."

Morten kissed me again and put his head on my chest afterwards. It was nice having a quiet morning in his arms. The kids were already awake. I could hear them in the bathroom. I closed my eyes and enjoyed the few seconds I had left.

"I'm glad that part is all over," Morten said. "Having young kids and all. I'm glad I'm not having any more of them."

"Me too," I said, holding him close to me.

I heard the kids in the hallway and pushed Morten off me. "I've got to get up," I said. "I need to prepare breakfast for the kids."

"Not now," Morten growled. "Can't we stay like this for a little longer...say, like forever?"

I got up from the bed and threw a sock at him. "No. Get up!"

Morten laughed and jumped out of bed. I put on some sweats, thinking I'd take a shower later, once the kids were off.

In the kitchen, Victor was already sitting on his chair, staring at the table. Brutus was sitting behind him like he was guarding his back.

"Good morning, buddy," I said, while putting bread in the toaster.

"Technically, you don't know if it is going to be a good morning or not until it's over," he answered.

"Wow, someone's in a good mood," I said.

"As a matter of fact, you're right. I am in a good mood."

I poured him some juice, and served it to him. Victor never got irony. "That's great, buddy. I'm glad you're in a good mood."

The toasted bread was done, and I buttered it for him and put some jelly on top and served it. Maya stormed in and threw herself on a chair. Morten followed.

"Any coffee yet?" he asked.

I looked at the coffeemaker. Water had started to run through. "Not yet. But soon."

"Why didn't you tell me Kenneth was killed?" Maya asked.

My heart dropped. I turned to look at her. "What?"

"Why didn't you tell me someone killed him?" she repeated.

"I...I...Where...Who told you he was killed?" I asked.

"Dr. Sonnichsen. She said yesterday that she couldn't believe anyone would do such a cruel thing to a poor little dog. She also said he was killed."

I stared at my daughter, baffled. Then I looked at Morten, who put his hands up, resigned. "Don't look at me. I haven't told anyone."

"So, it is true?" Maya said. "Why didn't you tell me? Who killed him? I want to know, Mom!"

The coffeepot finished and made a sound to let me know. I didn't react. I stared at my daughter, not knowing what to say or do. Something was fishy here. How did Dr. Sonnichsen know about this?

"I wanted to protect you," I said. "I didn't think there was any reason for you to know."

Maya scoffed. "That's so typical of you. Why can't you ever make a right decision in your life? I bet he was killed because of those things you've done, those things that everyone is talking about. Why is it that my life has to be so miserable just because of you? Everything bad in my life has something to do with you. It's not fair. I'm not the one who should be punished."

"I'm sorry, Maya. But we've all been victims here of this person harassing us. Morten has been suspended, I am facing some real serious charges, and you lost your dog."

"Why do I have to be dragged into all of this?" Maya said, tearing up. "Why did Kenneth? He never hurt anyone. Why does everybody around you have to suffer?"

Her remarks hit me right in solar plexus, and I felt tears welling up. I bit my lip to keep them back.

"I'm sorry, Maya. I really am."

Maya got up and pushed her chair backwards. "No, you're not. You don't care about anyone but yourself!" she said, grabbed her backpack, and stormed out.

I exhaled and leaned back. Morten poured me some coffee and put a hand on my shoulder. Victor had, as usual, not reacted to any of this. He was in his own little world while finishing his toast.

"So, this Dr. Sonnichsen, huh?" Morten said. "How well do we know her?"

55

JULY 1965

"You killed him! You killed him! Oh, God. Oh, dear God. You killed him! You really killed him!"

Jonna was still screaming when Ulrik finally came back to being himself. He looked at her terrified face, then at the lifeless faceless body on the carpet in front of him.

"Oh, my God," Peter said. He was sitting up on the bed. His body and face were badly bruised. "What are we going to do?"

Behind Ulrik, Per and Erling were whimpering and crying loudly, holding onto each other. Ulrik let the rifle fall to the ground, while feeling the urgency of the situation overwhelm him. If anyone found out he had killed the man, they would all be sent away. Ulrik, Peter, and Jonna were all old enough to be prosecuted. They would go to juvenile prison. Their lives would be ruined. They all knew, and now their eyes met as they understood the gravity of the situation.

"We need to get rid of him," Peter said.

Jonna nodded. "Peter's right."

Ulrik looked at both of them, then turned to look at the two young ones. "You two. You can help too," he said. "Get buckets of soap and water and help Jonna clean off the blood. Peter and I will get rid of the body."

He looked at his younger brother. Peter was shivering. When he moved, he was in pain. Still, he managed to get dressed and help Ulrik carry the remains of old Hansen out of the bedroom and down the hallway. They avoided each other's eyes as they carried him out into the yard. They put him on the grass. One of the dogs came running over and sniffed the body, but Peter shooed it away.

Ulrik found shovels, and they started to dig. It was getting darker out and the twilight soon covered them. They dug without sharing a word of even a look. Ulrik focused solely on the task of removing the traces of their deed, of his deed, and even though he wanted to, he never asked Peter a single question about how this had happened, or if this was something that had been reoccurring. He did, however, wonder for how long his brother had been a victim of this abuse from the old man. He wondered about the bruises he had seen on his brother's arms and back earlier this year that he had claimed had happened while working. But he never asked. The embarrassment on Peter's face told him he shouldn't.

When the hole was deep enough, they threw the body in, covered it in gasoline, and lit it on fire. They threw branches on top of it and let the fire burn out. It smelled awful. Once the fire died out, and the body was nothing but charcoal and bones, they covered it all with dirt. Ulrik's hands were shaking heavily as he put the final shovel full of dirt on top.

Lastly, they moved an old huge oil barrel from further down the yard, rolled it across the grass, and placed it on top of the grave. It seemed to cover the fresh dirt nicely.

They walked back inside and found Jonna and the boys finishing up. They had scrubbed the walls and floors down and managed to get rid of every trace. It looked so good, Ulrik almost felt like they were going to get away with this.

They had to. They simply had to.

Ulrik gathered everyone in a circle and looked into theirs eyes, one at a time. "This will be the last time any one of us ever speaks of this, do you hear me? It is never to be mentioned again. Not to anyone, not even each other!"

There was a short pause before everyone nodded. Ulrik stared particularly at Erling and Per to make sure they understood what he had said. He wasn't worried about Erling, since he was a troublemaker and used to keeping secrets from his parents to not get in trouble. But Per, he wasn't so sure of. Per shared everything with his mother. Ulrik had never known him to tell a lie in his life. Would he be able to keep this secret? Would he keep that big mouth of his shut?

The five of them rode their bikes back to the farm in silence, and when Ulrik asked Jonna if he should escort her home, she turned him down. She drove off, while his mother scolded him in the background for coming back so late with Per and Erling, whose parents were worried sick. He kept staring after Jonna, even long after she was gone, wondering if he would ever see her again.

56

NOVEMBER 2014

I called Dr. Faaborg immediately. He was the one who had referred Dr. Sonnichsen to me to help out Maya.

"Well, hello, Emma, dearest. How are things?" he said cheerfully, as usual. "You've certainly put yourself in the eye of the storm this time, huh? Well, I, for one don't care if you hacked anyone. I don't even care if you hacked the Queen. I love your books anyway. Any new ones on their way?"

"Yes, if I could just get my computer back," I said. "It's almost done, but I can't finish it, since the police confiscated my laptop."

"That's too bad. I'm sorry to hear that. I had hoped to get a signed copy."

I chuckled. Dr. Faaborg was my biggest fan. It warmed me. "You will. But that's not why I'm calling. I wanted to know a little more about this Dr. Sonnichsen you sent to me to work with Maya..."

"I'm gonna stop you right there. A doctor? I didn't refer any doctor, as far as I recall," he said.

Uh-oh.

"Dr. Sonnichsen," I continued, with a strange feeling inside of me. "You sent her to me to work on Maya getting her memory back?"

The doctor went quiet for a little while before he answered. "I've never heard that name before. This is very strange. You say he's a doctor?"

"She. She is an occupational therapist. She specializes in children with amnesia."

"Never heard of her. Sorry. You say I referred her to you?" Dr. Faaborg said, sounding very puzzled.

"That's what she told me," I said, getting more and more angry. This woman had been in my house every day for months now. I let her close to my daughter. I let her into my life. I couldn't believe this.

"I'm sorry," he said.

"No. I'm the one who's sorry," I said. "Sorry for being so incredibly naïve."

We hung up and I looked at Morten.

"Never heard of her, huh?" he said.

"Nope."

"Then who the hell is she?" he asked.

I shrugged and sipped my coffee. "Your guess is as good as mine. But now it all makes sense. If she's been spying on us in order to hurt us, that's why she was outside my house in the middle of the night on the night of the fire. I always thought I owed her for catching that crazy woman, but now I'm rethinking it. I always wondered what she was doing there at that time of night. It was strange."

"What about the hacking? Had you told her about that?"

"I never tell anyone. Except for you, of course. But she might have seen it on my computer or something."

"So, you think she sent me that email as well?" Morten asked. "The one with the link in it?"

"She must have. To frame you. And she killed Kenneth. Oh, I hate her for doing that. But that explains why none of the dogs reacted to her being here in the house. I bet she went in from the patio. She knows where I keep the spare key. I told her once, in case she arrived and we weren't home yet or something. I said she could always just walk in from the back and wait for us."

Morten exhaled. "How many times have I told you it's stupid to leave that key out there?"

"I know," I said. "It's just such a great help when Maya loses her keys, which she does constantly, or for Victor in case I get stuck in town and don't make it home in time. It's convenient for all of us."

"And for burglars and people like Dr. Sonnichsen who want to hurt you as well," Morten said sarcastically.

I drew in a deep breath. He was right. I shouldn't leave the key out there. Maybe if I put it in a different place?

I tried to gather my thoughts and wrap my mind around this discovery. If Dr. Sonnichsen didn't exist, if she hadn't been sent by Dr. Faaborg, then who was she? And why on earth did she want to hurt me so badly?

It was time I found out. I was done being a victim.

57

NOVEMBER 2014

Lisa's head was spinning with numbers and headlines from today's paper. She couldn't believe they could be so degrading towards her. How could they not agree with her on this important subject? She didn't understand it.

She grabbed a cart and stormed into SuperBrugsen. She had a few minutes to pick up some things for tonight's dinner before she had to be back at the office for another meeting. She hated grocery shopping on her lunch break, but it was the only chance she had in today's busy schedule. She was planning on making Goulash tonight.

She was going to make it the real Hungarian way with potatoes, so she hurried to the vegetables, found a bag of potatoes, carrots, bell peppers, and onions, and threw it in the cart before she hurried to the aisle with spices. She didn't have time to read the labels, but simply pulled down all the paprika she could find, then rushed to the next aisle to get some cereal for tomorrow morning, along with some milk and cheese. All that was left on the list now was canned tomatoes.

"Aisle six, by the canned vegetables," she mumbled to herself and looked at her watch. It was quarter past one. She had fifteen minutes to finish up here, drive all the way home with the groceries, and back to city hall to make it to her meeting. She had to hurry. It was the most important meeting of the month. This was the City Council's budget meeting. This was when they discussed how to spend the money. She had to be there. Especially now that there was no mayor. She would be able to get some of her most pressing matters pushed through. This was the time for her to show them she was capable of being in charge. Show them how it was going to be. Being late for a meeting like that showed a lack of character. It showed weakness. She couldn't do that. They hardly respected her as it was at city hall. But they were going to. Oh, yes, they were.

As soon as she won.

Lisa speculated like a crazy person, while pushing the cart through the aisles. She had to figure out a way to change people's opinion about her. She had to regain their sympathy, their trust. But how? She had only a few days left before the election. How was she going to turn it all around in that short of a time?

Well, she'd have to think about that later. Now, it was time to focus on making it to that stupid meeting. Oh, how she wished she didn't have to deal with all these amateurs in city council. They could drag out any matter for what seemed like eternity. All the paperwork just because she wanted to put up more trash cans in the city. She would have to change that in the future.

Lisa found aisle six and turned the corner, then she stopped. There she was again. In the middle of the aisle stood that Asian woman, her cart blocking the aisle. She was looking at some can, reading the label very thoroughly. Lisa sighed. Her canned tomatoes were on the other side. She had to get past this woman in order to get to them.

Maybe she'll move the cart once you get closer.

Lisa felt disgust as she walked with determined steps towards the Asian and her cart. The woman didn't react; she kept reading like it was the most important matter in the world. Lisa came closer, then stopped when she couldn't get past her. She cleared her throat. The woman still didn't react. She had that rat sitting on her shoulder. Lisa could have sworn it was mocking her, the way it looked at her. How was she even allowed to bring that thing in the store with her?

"Excuse me," Lisa said. "I'm kind of in a hurry here."

"Just a second," the Asian woman said. She turned her head and looked at Lisa with a huge smile. "Gotta read those labels. You never know what they put in those cans, do you? Gotta be careful these days. Can't have that gluten, and especially not wheat, now can we?"

Lisa sighed. She looked at her watch. "Well, no we can't," she said, trying to be polite. "I'm all into eating right and organic too, but I really can't be late either. So, could you please?"

"Now, eating organic isn't everything," the woman said. "You have to be careful with that as well. Read the labels, I always say."

"That's great, but could you maybe move your CART so I can get to my meeting?" Lisa said.

The Asian woman smiled again. "Always in a rush, are we?" she asked and finally moved her cart out of the way so Lisa could get past her. She growled and ran for the canned tomatoes. "Stupid Asians," she mumbled and pulled two cans down.

"Today's number is five; you do realize that, don't you?" The Asian woman yelled after her. "Gotta be careful on days that are five. Five can mean death or bad accidents."

Lisa froze with the can in her hand, and turned to look at the Asian woman. Then she smiled widely. Not her forced election smile, no, but a smile coming from deep within; a genuine smile, indicating that she was very very pleased at this moment. Pleased with the idea that had just popped into her mind, inspired by what the Asian woman had said.

A smile stating that she now knew exactly what to do to win this election.

58

NOVEMBER 2014

We knocked on the door to Dr. Sonnichsen's apartment, and rang the doorbell several times, but no one answered. I felt so furious, I could have exploded. Morten looked at me.

"She's not home. Do you want to wait for her to get back? Or should we come back later?"

I shook my head. "Neither. I want inside of her apartment. I want to invade her privacy the way she has invaded mine." I pulled out a screwdriver I had brought, just in case we ended up in this exact situation.

"No, Emma. Don't," Morten said when he saw it.

I didn't listen. I worked the lock and opened it with one smooth movement.

"Wow. Where did you learn to do that?" Morten asked.

"Same place I learned all the other criminal stuff," I said. "It comes in handy when you forget your key every now and then."

"Your ex-boyfriend? He sounds more and more sympathetic," Morten said, lifting his eyebrows.

"I know. He was bad company, but the sex was great," I said with a smile. Morten went pale.

"No, just kidding," I said. "He was awful, as a matter of fact. I was young. I liked the bad guys back then, but I knew I had to get out of there if I didn't want to live a life where I would only see my husband on Wednesdays during visiting hours, if you know what I mean."

Morten chuckled. I pushed the door open. He grabbed my shoulder. "Are you sure you want to do this? It is a serious offense. Breaking and entering. You know that. I can't protect you if you get caught. I'll go down with you. If anyone finds out, I'll never work as a policeman again. It's really bad."

"I know. But it's something I have to do. I have to find out who this woman really is, and I have a feeling she's not going to tell me willingly."

Morten closed his eyes and sighed. "That's probably right, but..."

"I'm already being charged with serious offenses. It can hardly get any worse, the way I see it," I said.

"But it can, Emma. It can get much worse."

"You stay here then. I'm going in," I said, and walked inside the apartment. Morten waited outside the door for a little while before he finally decided to follow me in. We walked into the living room and stopped.

"Wow," Morten said.

"I know."

The walls were plastered with articles and pictures of me. Some of the pictures had a red circle around my face and the words DIE written above it. It was really creepy. The number five was written everywhere, painted in big letters on the wall with red paint.

"Well, at least we're not wrong about this woman, huh?" I said, and walked over to the computer. I opened the lid and turned it on.

"I know I'm not allowed to be anywhere near a computer, but I crossed the line into being a criminal when entering this apartment anyway, so..." The screen opened and a picture of a big rat appeared as the background. I gasped and cupped my mouth. I had seen that rat before.

"I know this rat," I said with a small shriek. "I'm not sure, but..."

"Look what I found," Morten said, and picked something up from the top drawer of the dresser.

"A passport?" I said.

"Two, actually," Morten said, and showed me the name and the picture of the first. It was clearly Dr. Sonnichsen's. "Check the second one out," he said, and opened it. The picture staring back at me made my stomach turn.

"Dr. R.V. Devulapallianbbhasskar!!"

59

Three months had passed since the incident, and none of them had spoken of it since. Ulrik hadn't seen Jonna. He had looked for her at the library on the last Saturday of the month, but not found her there. He had tried to drive by her house a few times, but never tried to knock on the door. He had a feeling she didn't want to see him again.

Ulrik was getting anxious. The body of old Hansen hadn't showed up, but people had started wondering where the old man could be. Especially Ulrik's father, who had asked Peter to go down there on several occasions to check on the old man. Peter had done so without saying anything, but come back with the same message...that the old man wasn't there.

"That's strange," Ulrik's dad would say. "The old man never leaves his home. Not since his wife died."

When they had come home after burying old Hansen in his own yard, Peter had told their father that the old man didn't need his help anymore, and their father had taken it that Peter had misbehaved and been fired, since he had ended up with all those bruises. Their father had assumed it was Peter's own fault for not doing proper work or being rude to Mr. Hansen. Peter hadn't disagreed, but Per had wanted to defend his older brother. And every time it came up, how Peter had not behaved right at old Hansen's farm, Per had opened his mouth, and it was only because of Ulrik's look or because he interrupted at the right time that he hadn't said anything yet.

It worried Ulrik immensely. He wasn't sleeping at night and he constantly watched over Per to make sure he didn't accidentally spill the beans on them and ruin their lives. It had turned Ulrik into a nervous wreck. He had tried to talk to Per about it; he had tried to explain to him again and again that he had to keep that big mouth of his shut about what happened, or else...well, he had never figured out the proper threat yet, but something bad would end up happening if he didn't keep his mouth shut. That was sure.

But keeping the secret was hard on Per. Being only six years of age, Per was used to telling his mother everything. The two of them were extremely close. And the more time that passed, the more Ulrik worried that this would be the day when his big secret was revealed.

One day, they were sitting at the dinner table. Once again, their father brought up old Hansen and how odd it was that no one had seen him in months. Ulrik and Peter's eyes met across the table. It was rare that the two of them looked at each other, since they had avoided contact ever since that day, but whenever old Hansen came up, they did. Ulrik felt his hands shaking under the table. Peter bit his lip and blushed.

"Why are you boys hardly eating?" their mother asked. "Ulrik, you're getting too skinny. You're working yourself to death. You have to eat something."

"The boy is fine," their father said. "He's not the one I worry about. I worry about the other one over there," he said, and nodded in Peter's direction. "If he can't even keep a job...if he's rude and gets himself in trouble like he did at Mr. Hansen's, then what are we supposed to do with him? He's no good if he can't work. Is he going to live here forever? What worries me the most is the fact that he refuses to even tell me what it was he did that was so bad that Hansen had to give him a proper spanking before firing him. I simply don't under-stand why he won't tell me. Tell me, goddammit," their father yelled and hit his fist on the table.

They all jumped at the sound. Ulrik looked at Per, while breaking into a sweat. His hands were clammy, and it was hard to hold onto the silverware. He kept staring at his baby brother. He could tell how it tore the little boy up to not say anything.

"You're just no good, are you?" their father asked Peter.

Per opened his mouth to say something. Ulrik felt his heart stop.

"He didn't do anything bad, Daddy," Per yelled. "The old man is bad. The old man is very very bad...he deserved what..."

Before he could finish his sentence, Per was interrupted by a loud yell coming from Ulrik. Ulrik jumped to his feet and ran over to grab his baby brother and toss him to the ground. He held him down while Per yelled and screamed. Their mother started screaming as well.

"Get off your brother, Ulrik! You're hurting him!"

Ulrik let go of Per, whose face had almost turned blue, and that was when Ulrik realized he had been choking him. Ulrik stared into the eyes of his younger brother as he tried to catch his breath, and sensed something had broken between them. Something vital. Per no longer trusted his older brother, and Ulrik no longer trusted him.

60

NOVEMBER 2014

I couldn't believe what we had discovered. This was all very very strange. Could Dr. Sonnichsen and Dr. R.V. Devulapallianbbhasskar be working together? Were they both living here in this small apartment? Or, what was going on here?

My hands were shivering in anger as I examined the computer. Morten rummaged around the living room, opening drawers.

"I can't believe this!" I exclaimed. "She's been watching me. Look what I found. Morten appeared behind me, and I showed him what I had discovered. I showed him the videos, the many hours of recordings from my house. "She's been monitoring our every move."

Now I saw the anger in Morten's eyes as well. "What the hell is this? Did she put cameras up in your house or something?"

"Sure looks like it. That's how she knew I'd been hacking; that's the proof she claimed to have in the article on Facebook. I can't believe this. I feel so violated, so invaded."

"Tell me about it. I mean, she has footage of the two of us...?" Morten said, shocked.

"I know. It's really intimidating."

"It makes me so angry." Morten made a growling sound. "I can't believe this."

"The question is, what to do about it?" I said. "We need to figure out if she is any relation to Dr. R.V. Devulapallianbbhasskar, because she's a criminal and there's a warrant out for her arrest, am I right?"

"Yes, you're damn right. That's my case, but the woman left the country, according to our investigation. Traveled to Korea and never came back. How is she even in this country without our knowledge? She can't have come back by plane. I have her picture up in every airport in the country. Even Interpol is looking for her."

I leaned back in the chair, while looking at the two passports on the table. "Korea, huh?"

"Yes, we got her route from the travel agent who sold her the tickets. There was a return ticket, but she wasn't on board that flight."

"Hm," I said.

"What?" Morten asked.

"Could we check who else was on that flight? "

"You think Dr. Sonnichsen could have been on board instead? You can't just give someone your plane ticket, you know."

"Nah you're right. Plus Dr. R.V. Devulapallianbbhasskar's passport is here, so that means she must be too, right?"

Morten grabbed a chair and sat down next to me. "Yeah. I guess so."

I clicked on the doctor's mailbox and opened it. "But Korea. There's something that rings a bell for me about that place. Something I read recently. An article about how far they are in South Korea in the technology of transplantations and plastic surgery. Lots of Asian women travel to South Korea to get to look more like us here in the West. You know, the cheekbones, the bigger eyes, the rounder butt, the skin. They want to look like us. And they're so good at it down there that people have trouble entering their homelands afterwards, because they don't look like the picture on their passport."

"What are you getting at?" Morten asked. "I'm not sure I follow."

"What if someone came to them and asked them to do the opposite?" I asked.

"You mean, turn someone Asian?" Morten looked puzzled. "Is that really possible?"

"Why not?" I searched the emails, and quickly found several coming from a Korean address. "See here," I said. "This is a correspondence she's had with a Korean doctor. He's helping her get a new passport as well. See what he's written here. A name and an address. Plus, he asks her if she has experienced any pain since the operation. Look, she wrote back that she is very satisfied with the results, except the nose...she's a little concerned whether it looks real enough. It's still very swollen. It all makes sense, Morten. I always thought she looked a little off, that her skin was a little light and her face looked a little strange. But I figured she was only half Asian, that either her mother or father was Danish. I often wanted to ask, but never did."

"That's true. Now that you say it, I can totally see it. You really think she had her face changed?"

"And now she's here getting her revenge. It makes sense, Morten. We ruined her career by discovering what she was up to. Now she wants to get back at us. Oh, my gosh, I feel awful. I've had her this close to Maya this whole time! Maya, whom she held captive, whom she experimented on with drugs. What kind of a mother am I?"

Morten put his hand on my shoulder. "It'll be alright. But now I believe we must hurry out of here before she gets back. We have no idea what she might do if she finds us here."

"You're right. Just let me do one last thing." I pulled out a USB-drive and put it in her computer. Then I copied everything, all the videos, the emails, everything on the computer to the drive, and pulled it out. "There. If she tries to destroy the evidence, then I have a backup."

"I've always heard back-up is very important. Now, I finally understand," Morten said.

He had barely finished his sentence when my phone rang. It was my lawyer. "Michael has been beat up. It's bad," she said.

"How bad?" I asked anxiously.

"He'll live, but he's in the hospital. He says you and Morten did this to him. He says Morten threatened to kill him when he was at your house. Is this true? This is not good, Emma. He'll use it against you. Morten might be charged with attempted murder. His lawyer says the two men who beat him up told him they were sent by Morten. When the police in Copenhagen spoke to them, they told them they had been paid by Morten as well. It doesn't look good, Emma."

"But, Morten would never...I would never?"

"I hope not. But the evidence is pretty strong against you, Emma. It's getting harder and harder to defend you."

61

NOVEMBER 2014

She saw them leave the apartment building as she drove onto the street. She parked the car and shut the engine off to avoid attracting their attention. They looked angry. Both Emma and Morten walked with very firm and angry steps. It didn't take the numerologist many seconds to figure out that they had been to her apartment.

Her cover had been blown. They knew who she was. They weren't dumb people. They were annoying and irritating, and she hated their guts, but they weren't stupid. They knew who she was. If only she had gotten back a little earlier. If only she hadn't spent all that time talking to that stupid politician in the supermarket, then she would have gotten back earlier, maybe just in time to kill them both in her apartment. It wasn't how she had planned to take them down, but it would do.

Now, she had to come up with something completely different.

The numerologist sighed and looked at Misty, sticking out her little face from the purse on the passenger seat.

"I think you're right. We can't go home. It's too dangerous."

She watched as Morten and Emma drove off, and then started the engine. She had to get out of there. She decided to follow Emma and

Morten, to see if she could somehow come up with a great way to get rid of them, but as she watched them drive off to the police station, she stopped and turned the car around. This was worse than she thought. She had to think of something fast.

She drove back to Emma's house and parked the car far enough away for them not to see it when they came back. She walked into the backyard and found the spare key, where Emma always left it. She hadn't moved it yet, even after what happened to Kenneth. She really wasn't being very careful.

The numerologist let herself in and walked into the kitchen. She went through the drawers to find a knife or something else she could use as a weapon. Frantically, she pulled things out, but none of them were spectacular enough. She wanted Emma to be in pain when she stabbed her. She didn't want her to die immediately. She wanted her to look in her eyes and plead for the numerologist to kill her. She opened another drawer, when suddenly, she heard a sound coming from behind her. She gasped and turned to look straight into the eyes of the big dog.

"Brutus. You scared me," she said. "You gotta stop sneaking up on people like this."

But, as the numerologist looked into the eyes of the dog, she suddenly pulled back. There was something in the way he was looking at her with his white shining eyes that made her feel uncomfortable all of a sudden.

The dog let out a low deep growl, then raised the hairs on its back and showed its teeth.

"Brutus. It's me, Dr. Sonnichsen. Don't you remember me?"

The dog growled and soon cornered her. The numerologist's heart started to race.

"Come on, Brutus. You know me, don't you? You can't be mad at me for what happened to your friend, can you?"

The dog came closer and started barking. A deep intense bark that frightened the numerologist so much, she jumped up on the kitchen table with a small shriek. She sat on her knees while the dog growled and stared at her from the floor.

"Shush. Go away," she said, her voice shivering in fear.

But the dog didn't listen. It kept growling, and they stayed like that for a long time. Every time the numerologist tried to move, the dog got to its feet, growled and showed its teeth. So, the numerologist stayed still.

"You'll have to sleep at some point," she whispered. "All dogs sleep during the day. As soon as you close those big ugly white eyes of yours, I'll be down from here. And that kitchen knife over there will be the last thing you ever see. Just you wait."

62

NOVEMBER 2014

"We're telling the truth here, Allan. You've got to believe us. She's trying to ruin everything for us. She even had some guys beat up Michael, Emma's ex-husband, and made it look like I paid them to do it. But I didn't. I would never do such a thing. You've got to believe me."

Morten was pleading with his colleague. We had just finished telling him everything about Dr. Sonnichsen, and how she had framed us. I had even showed him what we had found on the computer and put on the USB-drive.

"First of all, shame on you, Emma. You know you're not allowed anywhere near a computer," Allan said. "Second of all, I do believe you. I've believed in your innocence all along, Morten. I haven't known you long, Emma, but Morten, I know. I've known you for more than ten years. I know you don't watch illegal porn on your computer. But I'm not the one you have to convince."

I looked at Morten sitting next to me in Allan's office. I could tell how much he missed being at the station.

"We know. But we're asking for your help," I said, and put my hand on top of Morten's. "We don't know where else to turn."

Allan drummed with his fingers on the desk. "I can understand that. It's a difficult situation, I have to admit. But I'm swamped with this case and..."

"The case of the two brothers?" I asked.

"The Larsen brothers, yes," Allan said. "I can't seem to crack this case open. I mean, we've arrested this kid, this Tommy Malthesen, who claims to have killed the man in his letter to your daughter, but he refuses to speak. All he does is sing this annoying tune when we try to interrogate him."

"What tune?" I asked.

"I don't know all of it, or where it's from, but it ends like this:

He has no face
  He hides with the trees
  He loves little children when they beg and scream...
  Please!

"Have you googled it?" I asked.

Allan looked puzzled. "No. Can't say I thought it was important."

"Well, try." I nodded towards his computer.

Allan shrugged. "Can't hurt, I guess." He tapped on the computer, and pressed enter. "I just put in the last lines, let's see what it comes up with. Ah, I see. It's a lullaby. Slendy's lullaby?"

"Slender Man," I said, and looked at Morten. "I had a feeling. So, you think Tommy Malthesen killed Ulrik Larsen as well?"

Allan shrugged. "I guess."

"But another knife was used to kill Ulrik Larsen," I said. "That one belonged to Jens Krohn. Whatever happened to him?"

"We had to release him," Allan said.

"What about Rasmus, his son?" I asked. "Did you ever question him about the murder?"

"I...we had him in here, yes. We asked him about the knife and whether he could have taken the knife. I didn't really think he could have done it."

"Hm," I said, and looked at Morten.

"I know that look," Morten said. "What are you thinking?"

"Mayor Bang's wife said there was a guy in her house on the night of the fire, right? He was dressed in a suit and tie and had no face, just like Slender Man. Two teenage boys connected to two other killings. Actually, it's three if you count in William Korsvig, whose bike was found near the mayor's house. There's something that doesn't add up here. What's the connection between the mayor and the two brothers?"

Allan shrugged. "I don't believe there is any connection. The two brothers have a clear connection, of course, but the mayor?"

"Wasn't there a third brother?" I asked.

"What?" Allan said.

"Yes, there was. I've been reading Helle Larsen's letters to my grandmother. Helle Larsen was her sister. She was also Peter and Ulrik Larsen's mother. She had three sons, not two."

63

NOVEMBER 1965

"WE NEED TO DO SOMETHING."

Ulrik looked at Peter. His hands were shivering when he bit his nails. He had been a wreck the last couple of months. They all had. Ulrik couldn't eat anything, nor could he sleep. He was constantly afraid of what Per might say. So, he had asked Peter, Erling, and Jonna to meet him for a walk on the beach. He hadn't seen Jonna since the day of the incident. It hurt to see her again, especially seeing how she looked at him now. So differently. Like she was disgusted by both him and Peter.

"Per will tell if we don't do something," Ulrik continued.

It was drizzling, and Jonna's hair was getting soaked. She was still beautiful beyond anything he had ever seen, but she had gotten older, he thought. It seemed like years had been added to her face since the last time they saw each other.

"I heard him last night with our mother," Ulrik said. "He asked if God knew everything. He asked if God could forgive murder. I don't think he can keep his mouth shut. That's why I have asked all of you to come here."

Ulrik looked at Erling. He was the same age as Per, but seemed so much older, so much more mature. Ulrik never worried about him telling anything. He was as scared as any of them. Plus, he was used to keeping secrets.

"So, what do you suggest we do?" Erling said.

"I think we need to scare him a little. Just enough to keep his mouth shut. Let him know we mean business. I mean, if he tells anyone about this, then it's all over. It's not just my life that get's ruined. It's all of our lives. Forget all your dreams for the future. Forget everything."

Erling and Jonna both looked serious.

"Do you really mean to tell me you want to hurt your own brother to shut him up?" Jonna asked. "You really have changed, Ulrik. Or maybe I just never really knew you."

"Shut up!" Ulrik yelled. "Do you think I enjoy this, huh? You think I'm happy about how everything has turned out? I did it for my brother, for crying out loud. The man was hurting him. I tried to protect him. I tried to protect any children he might come across in the future. The world is a better place without him."

"But he's our brother," Peter said. "Per is our brother."

"So what?" Ulrik said. "I'm not talking anything bad. Just a little scare, that's all. Make sure he doesn't speak about it ever again. I tried talking to him. I've tried everything, but he doesn't want to listen to me anymore. I'm afraid of what he might do. I'm so scared he'll get angry at me and rat me out. I don't think he fully understands how serious this is, how serious it will be if he tells."

Jonna and Peter looked at each other. Erling looked at Ulrik. "I'm with Ulrik on this," he said. "I can't have my life destroyed. I have big plans for my future. My dad was just elected to *Folketinget*. He's a very important politician. I want to follow in his footsteps when I grow up. I want to go into politics. I can't have a criminal record. My dad tells me every day. Keep your path clean, he says. Even just a minor misconduct, and they'll be able to dig it out. That's what he tells me."

Ulrik listened to the young kid talk about his future, and

wondered how he could be the same age as his younger brother. To be this clear about his future plans was truly amazing.

"Who else is with me on this?" Ulrik asked, looking at his brother and Jonna. "All of our futures depend on it. Remember that when you make your decision."

Jonna bit her lip. "Can you promise me he won't get hurt?"

"No one is getting hurt," Ulrik said. "Just scared a little."

She nodded. He could tell she was still debating within. Finally, she looked into his eyes. "I'm not happy about it, but okay. I'm in."

Ulrik turned to face his brother. His poor pale brother who had gotten really skinny lately. "Peter?"

"I don't like this, Ulrik. I really don't."

"We're all in the same boat here, brother. I just can't stay awake one more night wondering if Per is going to tell soon, wondering if I'm going to jail the next day. You know what I mean. I've heard you up at night as well. We need to have assurance here. We need to be able to move on with our lives."

Peter nodded. "Alright then. Count me in."

64

NOVEMBER 2014

"You're telling me there's a third brother?" Allan said. "I haven't heard anything about a third brother. Where is he now?"

I shrugged. "I don't know. I haven't read all the letters yet. But I'm sure you can find him somewhere in the system."

Allan tapped in the computer. I felt so jealous. I missed my computer so badly.

"I think you're right," he said. "I'll have to go and talk to him right away. Looks like he's in a home somewhere here on the island. He needs to know about his brothers. I'll go right away."

"And what about Dr. R.V. Devulapallianbbhasskar?" I asked. "Could you take her in for questioning?"

Allan sighed. "I don't know. You say she's not Dr. Sonnichsen? That she had her face changed. I...I need to think about it a little. She's Asian now, you say?"

"I know it's a little much to take in, but yes. As I told you, and as you can see by the emails, she had her face changed in Korea. I don't know if they'd tell you if you called down there and asked, but..."

"You know what? You've been so nice and helped me out a little here, so I'll do you that favor and look into it, okay? But now I really should go and talk to this Per Larsen and tell him what happened to his brothers."

We left the police station feeling down. Here, we had all this knowledge, and still we couldn't really get anyone to believe us. What were we supposed to do? What was this woman's plan anyway? To destroy us?

"Let's just go home," I said, as soon as we were back in the car. "I need to feed Brutus anyway. He's been home alone all day without a bite to eat. I completely forgot to give him food this morning. Poor creature."

Morten started the car. "He's probably found something else to gnaw on, like a chair or something."

"Well, that's not really his style," I said.

We drove back in silence. It wasn't until we drove onto my street that I broke it. "So, what do you make of this case, huh? I can't seem to figure out how it is all linked. But I feel like I'm so close."

"Well, maybe Allan will get something useful from the third brother," he said.

"Yeah, maybe."

As he parked the car, I immediately heard barking. I got out and slammed the door.

"Is that Brutus?" Morten asked.

"It sounds like him, but he never barks. Something has to be wrong." I started running towards the house, and went through the front door. In my kitchen, I found Dr. Sonnichsen sitting on the kitchen table, yelling at the dog, who seemed to have her cornered. When she saw me, she gasped.

"Well, well," I said. "If it isn't Dr. Sonnichsen, or should I say Dr. R.V. Devulapallianbbhasskar?"

"So, you know. What else is new? You can't prove anything anyway. Get the stupid dog to let me go."

"No, no," I said. "First, you tell me everything you did. Every little detail. I would like to know how you did it."

Dr. R.V. Devulapallianbbhasskar smiled. Suddenly, I recognized the old doctor behind the new face. It was creepy. I couldn't believe I hadn't seen it before. Her eyes gave her away.

"You mean how I changed my face? You mean how I planned to destroy you? How I made the Facebook page, how I sent the email with the dirty link to your little boyfriend, how I killed that little ugly dog of yours that wouldn't stop barking, how I paid two men to beat up your ex-husband and make them say were sent by Morten? Oh, it was so easy, Emma. You made it so easy for me."

Brutus growled like he had understood what she said. I wanted to yell at her as well. I felt so angry, but not as angry as Brutus, who looked like he would attack her at any moment. Morten picked up the phone and called Allan.

"Yes, she's here now. Okay." He hung up. "Allan is on his way back from the home. He'll be here in a few minutes."

Dr. Sonnichsen tried to move, but Brutus growled again. A few minutes later, Allan stood in the doorway. I pulled Brutus back, and Allan approached her. "So, this is the lady you've been talking about?"

Dr. Sonnichsen looked at Allan. "Thank you, dear Officer, for coming. These two have held me captive for several hours now. The dog there is crazy, and they're even crazier. Thank you for coming and saving me."

"Tell Officer Allan what you told us," I said.

"Tell him what? That your dog attacked me? That you rambled on about how I was out to get you, to frame you. I have to say, Officer, these two have lost their minds. As a doctor, I know these things. I should have seen it coming."

"They claim you're really Dr. R.V. Devulapallianbbhasskar, who is wanted by the police. Is that true?" Allan asked.

"Dr. what? That's a strange name. Never heard of anyone by that name. No, you have it all mistaken, Officer. My name is Dr. Sonnich-sen. No one would have such a crazy name. Everybody knows you never put an R before a V."

"Come on!" I yelled. "You just admitted everything to us. Now you're lying?"

Allan pulled me aside. "Emma. I can't really arrest her. I don't have anything plausible here. You have to give me something."

I was about to scream. The woman had just admitted everything, and now this? I couldn't believe it! She was really playing with us all, wasn't she?

"But the things from her computer?" I said, but I never finished the thought before Dr. Sonnichsen exploited the few seconds of us not paying proper attention. She jumped down from the kitchen table, reached over for a kitchen knife, and grabbed Brutus by the neck, holding the knife to his throat. Brutus growled, but she held him tight.

"One step closer, and the dog dies," she said, pressing the knife against his throat.

Knowing how much my son loved the dog, I felt my heart stop. Morten made a move.

"Don't," I said. "She's killed one dog before in this house. She will kill it. She's not kidding."

Allan pulled out his gun and pointed it at her. "Step away from the dog," he said. But Dr. Sonnichsen had another plan. She lifted the knife and threw it towards Allan. He pulled to the side to not get hit, and while he had the gun turned away, the doctor let go of the dog and ran. I screamed and yelled for someone to stop her, then ran after her, but she was faster than me. When I reached the back porch, she was long gone.

"Crap," I said.

Allan and Morten were right behind me. "It's okay," Allan said. "She won't get far. It's an island, remember?"

"So, you finally believe us?" Morten asked.

"I believe she's worth taking in for questioning," Allan said. "But I'm gonna need more proof eventually to keep her there. Do you think you can get that?"

"I think I might know how we can get that," I said.

"You do?" Morten looked at me, puzzled.

"Yes. I do. The cameras. Remember, she planted cameras in my house? Well, my bet is they also recorded her confession just before Allan arrived."

"Oh, my God, I hope you're right," Morten said.

65

DECEMBER 1965

All he wanted was to get his kitten. It was getting dark on this day in December not long before Christmas, and Per was worried about his kittens. His favorite cat on the farm, old Martha had given birth to five of them just a week ago, and they gave the boy so much joy. He played with them every afternoon when he returned from school. They crawled on his body, and when he tried to walk away, they would hang on to his legs with their little tiny claws and make the cutest sounds. He simply adored them.

But Per had always been that way with animals. He liked them a whole lot better than he liked people. Especially lately. Especially after that day at old Hansen's farm. That was when Per had realized he really didn't like people a whole lot. Not even his own two brothers. He understood why Ulrik had been so angry. He understood why he felt like killing the old man, but he didn't understand why he insisted on keeping it all a secret. Why didn't anyone tell their father that it wasn't Peter's fault that he had lost the job? Per didn't like the way their father talked to Peter and told him he was good for nothing and that he would never amount to anything. That's why he wanted so badly to tell his parents the truth. To clear Peter, to make their father like Peter again. That, and to finally tell someone what had happened. Per couldn't bear to have to keep this secret. It was so hard, and it tore at him every day. It was almost painful. His mother had begun to suspect that something was going on. She could see it in her baby boy's eyes. She asked him often if everything was okay between him and his brothers. Especially after that night when Ulrik had attacked Per during dinner. That was when Per had stopped trusting his oldest brother. And he had a feeling that Ulrik didn't trust him either. Per was afraid of what he might end up doing to all of them.

So, he had finally decided to tell his mother. He would do it tonight when she had him come inside. He would tell her everything. Just get it off his chest. He didn't like keeping secrets. It gave him a bad feeling in his stomach and made him not want to laugh and play.

All this was on Per's mind when he saw the smallest of the five kittens had run off towards the big road. It looked like it was going for the forest on the other side. Per got to his feet and walked after it. But the small kitten was faster than he had expected, and he had to run a little to get it. It managed to run way into the road before he finally grabbed it. He checked for cars before he ran out there and grabbed it in his hands. He held it for a second and petted it on the back.

"Don't do that again," he whispered. "It's dangerous out here."

That was when the car hit him. It came from his right side. That was all he could tell. It hit him with a huge force and threw him into the air before he landed on his head on the asphalt. He didn't lose consciousness, but no one could tell. He heard the tires screech on the car that had hit him, then he heard it back up before he heard car doors opening and steps approaching. He saw their faces, but they didn't know he could see them.

"Is he dead?" Jonna asked, terrified.

A cold finger was placed on his throat. His brother Peter's face was close to his. "No," he said, relieved. "There's a pulse."

Then, his brother waved a hand in front of his face. "He's not blinking," he said.

"He looks dead," Erling said.

"Oh, my God, we killed him," Jonna cried.

Ulrik slapped her across the face. "He's not dead," he yelled at her. "Didn't you hear that he had a pulse?"

Jonna cried. So did Erling. "This wasn't how it was supposed to go," Erling whined.

Ulrik slapped him as well. "Pull yourself together!"

"You said he wouldn't get hurt!" Peter yelled at Ulrik.

"How was I supposed to know that he would run onto the road?" Ulrik yelled back, his voice cracking. "How? The plan was to get him in the car and take him to the forest, then beat him up and leave him there, remember? This wasn't part of the plan. It was an accident, goddammit."

"Well, you finally silenced him," Peter said, with tears in his eyes. His voice was trembling in anger and frustration. "Are you happy now? Are you?"

66

NOVEMBER 2014

Maya and Victor both came home shortly after officer Allan had left. He promised they would catch Dr. Sonnichsen some way or another.

"There aren't that many places she can hide on the island. We'll get her," he said to assure them, right before he drove off.

I wasn't all that convinced that he was right. She had managed to vanish before, and had tricked the police more than once.

"I'm going to my room. Dr. Sonnichsen will be here any minute," Maya said, as she came into the kitchen and threw her backpack on the floor.

"About that..." I looked at her backpack on the ground, and Maya saw it. She picked it up with a sigh.

"Dr. Sonnichsen won't be coming anymore," I continued, as the backpack was picked up.

"What? Why?" Maya said annoyed. "What did you do?"

"Why do you always assume that I am the one destroying everything?" I asked.

She shrugged. "Because you usually are. It's always your fault. You're ruining my life!" Her voice was breaking as she spoke. I could tell everything had been a little much for her lately, and decided she didn't need to know the truth about Dr. Sonnichsen, the only person she had trusted the last several months. It would simply break her heart to know that Dr. Sonnichsen had been the one to kill her dog. She didn't need that right now.

"So, why isn't she coming anymore?" Maya asked with a frown.

I looked at my beautiful almost-grown daughter, tilting my head to the side. "I guess she felt you're done. You've regained most of your memory, and she told me you needed to get on with your life."

Maya looked appalled. "And she didn't even say goodbye?"

"She was in a hurry."

That wasn't a lie, I thought to myself.

Maya stomped her feet on the floor with a loud groan. "Arrrgh. Why are grown-ups always so lame?"

Then she stormed upstairs and slammed the door to her room. I shrugged and looked at Morten, who had hid his face behind the newspaper. He had a smirk on his face. "That went about as well as when I speak with my teenage daughter. You're sure you don't want her to know the truth?"

I shrugged. "Maybe. I don't know. I just can't bear to see her heart-broken again. She just regained trust in grown-ups by spending time with the doctor. You can say what you want about her and why she was really here, but she certainly helped Maya get better. I am thankful for that, despite everything else."

Morten looked at the clock. "I should get home and spend some time with Jytte too. I think I'll take her out to dinner tonight."

I kissed his forehead. "I think that sounds like an excellent idea. You're always welcome to bring her here, if you like. I would like to bring our families together at some point."

Morten nodded, then kissed my lips. "I'll talk to her about it. But tonight I think we'll make it a father-daughter thing. But maybe tomorrow night?"

I chuckled and kissed him back. That was always his answer. I knew it wasn't his fault. Jytte just didn't want to accept the fact that he was seeing someone, and she certainly didn't want to meet my family. I had to accept that. At least for now.

"See you later, gorgeous," Morten said and left.

Victor was playing with Brutus in the yard and I watched them for a little while, still amazed at the connection between the two of them that seemed to be out of this world.

I sat on the couch in the living room, missing my computer. I grabbed my iPad and scrolled through today's newspapers that all declared Lisa Rasmussen to be a racist after her blunder on stage. I couldn't stop laughing. She was truly something, that Lisa, but part of me was happy she had a worthy opponent now, and I was definitely going to vote for Jonna Frederiksen after this. I threw a glare around the room, and my eyes stopped on the box of letters on the dresser. I hadn't had time to read them all. I wondered about the third brother. I had asked Allan about his visit earlier today, and he had told me Per Larsen was sitting in a wheelchair, and that he was severely autistic. He was lost to the world, the staff had told him, and he was unable to understand anything. Officer Allan had told him about his brothers anyway, since he had to, but the man sat in his wheelchair, drooling on himself, and didn't react at all. He had been living in the home his entire life. The nurse had also told Allan that the family hadn't visited him for as long as she had worked there, and she heard stories that they never did. Only the mother came once for Per's tenth birthday, many years ago, but she never returned.

"It was pretty sad," Allan said.

I picked up the box of letters, wondering how that young boy I had heard about in previous letters as this boy filled with life and happiness, how he had ended up like that. Carefully, I opened the last letter in the pile and started reading.

67
_____

JANUARY 1966

D<small>EAR</small> S<small>ISTER</small>,
    I am afraid I have some terrible news. A terrible tragedy has struck our family. I can hardly believe it. My hands are shaking as I write this to you, so you must excuse my bad handwriting. Three weeks ago, Per was hit by a car, and was admitted to the hospital in Esbjerg. We haven't been able to visit him much there, since it is very expensive and a long trip to the mainland for us. But we went yesterday, and they told us Per's brain was damaged when the car hit him, and he will never be the same. Oh, sister. I am heartbroken. I couldn't believe this was the same little boy that brought me such joy over the years. He was lying in the bed at the hospital, all lifeless. They say he can hear what I say, but not understand it. They say he is retarded. The blow to his brain made him retarded and unable to take care of himself. I am crying as I write this, because this tragedy has hit our family very hard. Not only have I lost my beloved Per, who will now have to live in a home, they say, but I am losing my two other sons as well. Ulrik was driving the car that hit Per, and Peter was in it with him. So were Jonna Frederiksen and Erling Bang. The boys haven't been the same ever since. Peter left the day after the accident. He

packed his suitcase and told me he was going to live in the city. He has dropped out of school and is working as a carpenter at the local lumber company in Nordby. Ulrik is going away too, he says. He can't stand it here anymore, he told me this morning. Claes is furious, but I sense it is no use to try and talk sense into him. Ulrik has made his decision. He's leaving the farm, and with both of the other brothers gone, there is no one to take over the farm when Claes wants to retire. He's heart-broken. We all are. Seeing Per in that hospital bed, unable to speak to me, was heartbreaking. At first, they thought he would get better, but they no longer believe he will. They told me to forget the boy I once knew...to pretend he has died.

"You've lost your son," Mrs. Larsen, the doctor said. "Forget about him. Try to have another child. That will make you forget about him."

But how can I forget about the most precious creature I have ever known? How am I supposed to forget him when I still love him? When I sense deep in my soul that he is still in there somehow? I swear, I thought he understood what I told him yesterday. I spoke to him for hours and told him everything that was going on at the farm, and I am certain he understood it. I could see it in his beautiful eyes. The doctors believe I'm just imagining it because I am mourning his loss, but the way he looked at me, I think he's still in there. He's still my little boy.

But now, they've taken him away. They've moved him to a home somewhere on the island and told me to not come visit since it will only *make my mourning harder on me*. It's best for everyone that I forget. Everyone seems to think so. Even Claes. He thinks we should try for another son, but I don't know if my old body can take any more. I don't know if I can?

Dearest sister. I am so sorry to have to bring you all this bad news. I hope you are well in the city.

Kind regards,

Helle

68

NOVEMBER 2014

I was crying as I read the last lines of Helle Larsen's letter to my grandmother. This was terrible. What a devastating tragedy. I put the letter on the table and looked at Victor playing in the yard. I wondered about him and his diagnosis of *mild autism*. I was suddenly very grateful that it wasn't worse than that. I knew he would never have a normal life, but at least he didn't have to spend it in a home somewhere in a wheelchair. At least he could play outside; at least he went to school along with other children. His life would be harder than most people's, yes, but I had a feeling he would be all right somehow. There were days I worried more about him than others, but I had a feeling deep down inside that he would figure out how to deal with this. He would get by.

I wondered about the two brothers and them being murdered like this. Why were they being killed? I couldn't stop thinking about the fact that Erling Bang had been in the car as well. There was, after all, a connection between the three of them. They had known each other as children.

I didn't get to finish the thought when Sophia stormed through my front door. She looked upset.

"Christoffer is gone!"

"What do you mean gone?" I asked.

"They called from school and told me he didn't come to class today, and he's not at the house. I've called all of his friends, not that he has that many, but none of them have seen him all day."

"When did you see him last? This morning?" I asked.

"Yes. He ate breakfast with the other kids and they rode off to school like they always do. Josephine tells me he parked his bike close to hers and then went inside the school, but his teacher says he never showed up. I need your help to find him."

"Of course," I said. "Do you want to just drive around, or do you have any ideas where he might have gone to. Does he have like a special place he likes to go to?"

Sophia looked confused. "I...I have to be honest and tell you I don't know. He's my oldest and therefore mostly takes care of himself while I'm busy with the young ones, you know? Christoffer is the one who takes care of most things himself. He's eleven. He's my easy child. I never have any trouble with him. He spends most of the day on the computer."

I called Victor and asked him to come inside.

"Have you seen Christoffer today?" I asked, when he and Brutus came running. Victor shook his head without looking at me.

"No."

"Not even at school?"

He shook his head again. "He skips school sometimes to be on the computer," he said.

I looked at Sophia.

"Really?" she said. "I didn't know that."

"Only when you're at work," Victor said.

"Maybe we should take a look at that computer of his," I said. "We need to see what he's been up to lately."

I took Victor and Brutus with me over to Sophia's house across the street. All of her kids were running around the living room and jumping on the couch; the twins were playing soccer inside. My head was about to explode after just a few minutes inside her house.

"The computer is in his room," she said, and showed us inside and closed the door to shut out the noise from the screaming kids. "Here. My mother gave it to him a year ago. She thought he needed it to get ahead in school. He's been on it ever since. I can't drag him away."

"*Minecraft?*" I asked and touched the mouse so the screen turned on.

"Yeah. All the kids play that now, right?" Sophia said, looking at Victor.

"Not Vic," I said. "He likes it outdoors. Don't you, buddy?"

Minecraft was already on. Sophia looked at me with a shrug. "I don't know anything about this."

"I'm not allowed to touch a computer," I said, thinking I didn't want to risk anything again. Allan had been very angry at me for touching Dr. Sonnichsen's computer. I could get in serious trouble for this. "Court's orders."

Sophia exhaled. "I guess I'll have to try then. Could you guide me?"

"I guess there's no harm in that. As long as I'm not touching the computer," I said.

Sophia was about to sit down by the computer, when Victor stepped up. "Can I try?"

I looked at him, puzzled. He had never shown any interest in computers. "No, Victor, I don't think…"

Sophia moved away from the computer. "Let him. I'll just break something."

"I really don't think…" I didn't get to finish the sentence before Victor was sitting in front of the screen, his fingers dancing across the keyboard. I dropped my jaw. I had never seen him this focused. He tapped and clicked, then wrote something. I walked up behind him and realized what he was doing was very advanced. So advanced I didn't even know what he was up to. Numbers and letters danced across the screen. I was truly impressed.

Victor stopped. "There," he said. "Christoffer has been talking to the same guy inside *Minecraft* for the past three months. I recovered all their chats. He adopted Christoffer in August."

"Adopted?" Sophia asked. "What does that mean? You're freaking me out here. What do you mean he was adopted?"

"You can get adopted in *Minecraft*," I said. "If they adopt you, you become part of their family. Maya does it all the time."

"This guy has adopted many others," Victor said. "He's very good at protecting himself, so I couldn't find anything on him, but I found the profiles and IP-addresses on all of the kids he adopted, then found their real names and addresses."

"How on earth did you do that so fast?" I asked, puzzled yet slightly proud, and very impressed.

"I used a trace route tool that I just invented. You wouldn't understand."

"What?"

"Here are their names and addresses. They all live around here," Victor said, and left the computer. I stared at the screen. "I didn't even know you had ever used a computer before?" I asked, looking at my son.

"I haven't."

We read through the chats with great concern. Apparently, Christoffer had been chatting with this guy about becoming one of his so-called proxies. It had started out with the man contacting him, asking if he wanted to be adopted; then, when he accepted, they started talking about his family. Word for word, we read how Christoffer felt...like no one cared about him in his family, how he felt lonely, how there was never any time for him, and this man, this guy who called himself Slender Man told him he could be his father if he liked, he could give him a family. He would care for him and could be the father he needed. He told him about the other kids he had adopted and made part of his family. There was just one thing, one little favor

Christoffer needed to do in order to be one of them, to be accepted into the family.

He had to kill someone.

"Are you kidding me?" Sophia said, when she reached the line where he told Christoffer that he expected him to do it.

"How...how did I not see this?" Sophia asked, with tears in her eyes. "I mean, my son...my poor son has been so lonely in this house. And I didn't know. What kind of a mother have I been? Why haven't I kept an eye on him on that computer? I didn't know he could get himself in trouble like this. I had no idea. And now this? My son is no murderer. He can't kill anyone. Do you think he would do it? For what? To become one of them? I don't understand."

I exhaled deeply while looking at the other names on the list Victor had found for us. I recognized all of them. Rasmus Krohn, William Korsvig, and Tommy Malthesen. All were the teenagers that had showed up in the investigation of the killings. So, this guy had made them all kill by promising them a new family? Was it really that easy? Apparently, it was. Apparently, Christoffer had been so hungry for grown-up company, for a male-role model that he was willing to do anything. This guy was really good. He knew how to push all the right buttons to get to the boy. He told him exactly what he needed to hear. It was really creepy to read how he slowly reeled him in and persuaded him to do this, telling him to trust him and that he would understand one day. For now, all he needed was to know his loyalty was really with Slender Man. This was how he would show him. This was how he became one of them. He made Christoffer plead to be accepted. He made it something Christoffer dreamt about and longed for, something he, in the end, lived for. Something worth killing for.

I decided I no longer cared about getting caught using a computer and sat at the keyboard. I went through Christoffer's emails and found an online order for a Slender Man costume from an online store. This was it. That was the last proof we needed to know what he was up to.

"We need to find him before he does anything stupid," I said.

"But where do we look?" Sophia asked. "It might already be too late?"

"The name of the person he's supposed to kill is here on the bottom. Jonna Frederiksen," I said as I looked up at Sophia. "It doesn't say when or where."

"Isn't that the woman who is running for mayor now?" Sophia asked.

"It is. And I have a feeling I know why this is the person supposed to go next."

"What do you mean?" Sophia said.

"I'll explain later," I said. "Right now, we need to find Christoffer before he finds her."

69

NOVEMBER 2014

They had agreed to another debate. A late afternoon debate on the main square of town at Lisa Rasmussen's request. She wanted to be able to explain herself properly to the public before the election, she had told the editor in chief at *Fanoe Times*, which was the newspaper that arranged the debates every year. At first, the editor had completely rejected her request, but Lisa Rasmussen had taken the man's stapler and stapled him in the forehead until he agreed to do it. She had given him one of her election smiles, then told him if he ever wrote a bad word about her in the paper again, she would make sure her daughter Amalie never talked to his daughter Maria again. They went to the same school, and Amalie was the most popular girl there. She was the one everyone wanted to be friends with. Amalie had the power to make his daughter's life a living hell, Lisa told him.

Now, she was standing behind the heavy curtain on the scene where, in about half an hour, the debate with Jonna Frederiksen would once again take place. But this time, it would be different. Lisa had a little something up her sleeve that was going to make sure she won this time.

If only Merethe did her part, then nothing could go wrong. But where was she? Why hadn't she arrived with Lisa's package yet? It had been quite an unusual request. Lisa knew that it was a lot to ask of her campaign manager, but she didn't think it was too much. After all, the dear campaign manager hadn't exactly delivered the results Lisa was paying her for, had she? No, Lisa didn't think it was too much to ask, but she had still made sure to make Merethe understand that she meant business. She had taken a picture of Merethe's son standing in front of his preschool, then told her that she would poke his eyes out with a needle if she didn't do as Lisa told her to.

Sometimes it was just too easy.

A few people had already gathered in front of the stage. Lisa had a feeling a lot more would come this time around. She had asked Merethe to stand in front of the local supermarket and hand out fliers announcing the debate before she went to get Lisa's package. Lisa looked into her purse and saw the gun. She had bought it many years ago from someone selling it out of his truck. It wasn't registered anywhere, and no one knew it belonged to her. She knew it would come in handy one day. She had just never known it would be like this.

"I'm back!" Merethe was panting. Her face was so pale, her teeth dirty, Lisa thought, and cleaned her own with her tongue to make sure none of this morning's romaine lettuce and kale smoothie was stuck between her teeth.

"Did you get what I wanted?" Lisa asked.

Merethe nodded. How did her hair manage to always get so greasy? Lisa frowned. People were just so...so unsanitary.

"Good. And she's out there in the crowd?" Lisa asked.

"The package is delivered, the eagle has landed," Merethe said, trying to sound clever. "I found her walking up from the beach. I did as you told me and paid her five hundred kroners to come to the debate."

"Good. Money always talks. Now, take my purse and go out and do your job. Don't let me down," Lisa said, and pulled out a needle from her pocket and poked it in the air towards Merethe to show her what would happen to her son if she didn't do as she was told. Merethe whined and grabbed the purse. Lisa burst into loud laughter when she saw the look on Merethe's face. It was just too funny.

Lisa cleared her throat just as her opponent Jonna Frederiksen showed up. She looked older than last time. She was smiling widely as she approached Lisa.

"So you wanted a rematch, huh?" she asked.

Lisa chuckled. "Not that I need it, old lady, but yes. I have asked to be heard once again. This time, you won't know what hit you. This time, I will win."

The old lady laughed. Lisa imagined grabbing her around the neck and just strangling her right there. She fought the urge.

"Well, we'll see about that," Jonna Frederiksen said. "Good luck."

"Oh, I don't need it."

70

NOVEMBER 2014

"They're having another debate downtown."

I looked at Sophia. We had been all over town looking for Christoffer and Jonna Frederiksen when we found a small notice on the ground telling about the debate. I looked at my watch.

"It's about to start. We have two minutes."

Sophia followed me as I ran up Main Street towards the square. I was panting heavily, and realized I was in worse shape than I had thought. I had called Morten and Allan while in the car and told them to look for Christoffer as well. I was so afraid of what he might do. It would simply ruin his life.

"We gotta hurry," I said, gasping for breath.

We ran into the square just as the editor of *Fanoe Times* took the stage and started talking to the many people that had arrived. I was quite surprised at how many had shown up for this event, even though it was a last minute thing.

Morten came running towards us, waving his arms. "They're starting now," he yelled.

"I know," I said.

All three of us hurried towards the stage and stood in the back while the editor in chief presented the two candidates. Everybody clapped when he said their names, and seconds later, Lisa Rasmussen and Jonna Frederiksen stepped out. Lisa was waving like she had already won the entire election. She was smiling like the picture on her posters and moving her arms like she thought everybody had come just for her.

I spotted Officer Allan joining the crowd as well, then glanced around me to see if I could spot Christoffer anywhere, or if I could see anyone wearing a Slender Man costume.

"Any news?" Officer Allan asked when he approached us.

On stage, Jonna Frederiksen had started her speech. A few people in front of me shushed us.

"I can't see him anywhere," I said.

"You really think that little kid is capable of killing someone?" Allan whispered.

"I didn't until I read all the online chats. This guy is very good. He knows how to push the right buttons on these kids."

"So, you believe the others were killed by the teenagers? Each one a different killer?" Allan asked.

"Yes. And all the victims knew each other. They were all in the car that hit Per Larsen."

Allan looked surprised. "Wow. I didn't know that."

"I read it in a letter from Helle Larsen to my grandmother. After the accident, Per Larsen's life was completely ruined."

"Yeah, well I saw him. He's in bad shape," Allan said.

"He wasn't until the car hit him," I continued, while Jonna Frederiksen made some excellent points on stage and people started clapping. I looked at Lisa Rasmussen. She looked completely unmoved. She was still smiling like she had won the whole thing.

"I see," Allan said. "So we might be looking at a revenge-motive here?"

"It appears so. It's a little too coincidental that three of the four in that car are now dead, and we know that someone has persuaded Christoffer to kill the last."

"I see what you mean," Allan said. "But who the heck is telling these kids to do these things? Who is this Slender Man?"

"That's the big question," I said. "It can't be Per Larsen. Maybe his parents? Whatever happened to his mother and father?"

"They're both dead. Ulrik Larsen's daughter told me they died ten years ago. She said that only Peter Larsen was left. Apparently, she knew nothing about Per Larsen's existence."

"Could she have done it?" I asked.

Jonna Frederiksen was done with her speech and the crowd started clapping. I spotted Dr. Sonnichsen. She was standing very close to the stage. I pulled Allan's arm and pointed. He nodded to let me know he had seen her. I smiled. This time, she couldn't get away.

"I'll grab her as soon as the debate is over," Officer Allan said, just as Lisa Rasmussen took the stage.

71

NOVEMBER 2014

She thought she had found the best hiding place in the world. The numerologist knew the ground was burning under her feet, and had run along the beach thinking she could make it to the ferry before the police got to her, but when she reached the harbor she saw the police car parked and two officers checking all the cars that wanted to leave the island. There was no way she could get over to the other side right now. She had to hide somewhere on the island till it got dark, then find a boat or something and try to get to the mainland on her own. She had thought about many places to hide, when this strange woman had approached her and asked her to come to the debate and said she would even pay her five hundred kroner to do so. It suited the numerologist perfectly, since she would be able to hide for a little while in the crowd, and she really needed the cash. Cash was untraceable, and with five hundred kroners, she could get to Germany. They would never find her there. The numerologist wondered about the numbers. They hadn't been in her favor this morning. She had known something would go wrong. She had never imagined that it would go this wrong, though. It annoyed her immensely that her plan had backfired. All because of that stupid dog. She really wasn't happy about having to leave the island without having finished what she came here to do. But it was too dangerous for her to stay. She really wanted to kill Emma Frost, but she didn't want to be caught doing so. She didn't want to spend the rest of her life in jail. It would be better to come back in a few months and finish it. It would be more of a surprise that way. At least she had managed to make her suffer. That would do for now.

The strange woman who had given her the money was standing next to her and was now cheering wildly as the second candidate took the stage. The numerologist laughed when she saw this Lisa Rasmussen take the microphone. She was smiling so strangely and so confidently, which was so odd, since no one seemed to like her or clap for anything she said. But the numerologist didn't care. All she wanted was a cover right now, as the police were looking for her everywhere.

The woman next to her smiled oddly at her, and the numerologist felt a strange sensation in her body. She didn't like the aura surrounding this woman or Lisa Rasmussen. There was an energy field surrounding those two that was off. Something was up with them, and it wasn't nice.

The woman grabbed her purse and pulled something out, then handed it to the numerologist. The numerologist looked down at what she had in her hand. It was covered in a napkin.

"Here," she said, and pushed it at the numerologist. "Take it."

"I'm not taking that," the numerologist said, looking down at the gun that the woman tried to push at her.

"Take it!" the woman said.

"No, I won't!" the numerologist yelled so loudly that Lisa Rasmussen stopped talking on the stage.

"Is something wrong down there?" she said.

It happened so fast that the numerologist had no idea how it happened. Suddenly, the woman yelled:

"Gun, she's got a gun!"

The woman then pressed the gun into the numerologist's hand

and, while both their hands were on it, she fired the gun at Lisa Rasmussen, who fell backwards with a loud scream.

"Help! It's an assassination attempt! Help!"

Then, the woman let go of the gun and it fell to the numerologist's feet. She then threw herself at the numerologist as the crowd scattered and people started screaming. Seconds later, Officer Allan was on top of her, holding her down, while the numerologist yelled:

"I'm innocent. I didn't do it!"

But the many people yelling and screaming as they fled the scene drowned her screams out.

72

NOVEMBER 2014

I couldn't believe what had happened. Dr. Sonnichsen had tried to assassinate Lisa Rasmussen? How strange was that? I had no idea she was after her as well. Why? As I drove back to the house with Sophia and Morten, I wondered what she was up to, and if she had just simply completely lost it. Lisa Rasmussen had been hit in the shoulder and was being taken to the hospital, while an officer had escorted Jonna Frederiksen away to keep her safe.

"We still haven't found Christoffer," Sophia said. "I have no idea where he is or what he's up to. I feel so bad for him, Emma, I really do. He must be so lonely."

I drove onto our street, and as I came closer to my house, I spotted someone sitting under the big oak tree on the lawn. Victor and Brutus were sitting next to him.

Sophia gasped. "Christoffer!"

I hardly managed to park the car before she jumped out and ran towards him. Morten and I both followed her and watched as she threw herself at him. Christoffer was crying and hiding his face between his hands. Victor and Brutus just sat next to him in silence.

"My God, Christoffer, are you alright? Have you done anything? Have you, kid? Have you done it?"

Christoffer shook his head. "I'm so sorry, Mom."

"Sorry for what, kid? Did you do it? You didn't kill her, did you?" Sophia asked.

Christoffer opened his backpack and pulled out the costume. Sophia looked confused. Christoffer shook his head. "I couldn't do it, Mom. I thought about it all day and rode around on my bike with the costume in my backpack, but I knew I couldn't do anything like this. There was no way. I'm such a failure, Mom."

"Oh, my God, no, son. You're not a failure. You have no idea how smart you are. I knew you would know better. I just knew you would." Sophia wouldn't let go of him. She hugged him and held him close. Then, she slapped him gently on the hair. "But don't ever scare me like this again. You hear me?"

"I'm sorry, Mom. It was just...well the other kids in the game did it. They all bragged about how they had done it, and I was the only one who hadn't...I wanted so badly to be more like them. I wanted to be one of them. They kept encouraging me to do it, and told me how fantastic it was."

Sophia slapped him again. It wasn't hard. "Don't ever strive to be part of a group that does things you don't want to. And no more computers for you for a long time, young man. You hear me?"

Sophia grabbed Christoffer around the shoulder and they walked home. I looked at Victor and Brutus, who were both staring at the ground. They were just so alike, those two, it was almost scary. But Brutus had certainly proved himself worthy as a member of our little family.

"Let's go inside," I said.

Victor, Brutus, and Morten all followed me, and I made hot chocolate for all of us, even though it was dangerously close to dinnertime. "What about Jytte? I asked Morten. "Weren't you supposed to cook for her?"

Morten nodded. "Yeah, but she decided she would rather hang

out with her new best friend Amalie from her school. She's suppos-edly the biggest thing since sliced bread around here. So, I guess you're stuck with me again tonight."

I chuckled. "I guess I can't complain about that."

I made a wonderful dinner, and we had a nice evening together, even though Maya was still pretty angry with me. I didn't care much. I just enjoyed knowing that Dr. Sonnichsen was behind bars and was going to stay there for a long time. It had been awhile since I had last felt this relaxed. Only one thing still bothered me. Even though we knew about the teenagers and what they had done, and I had told Allan to investigate it, we still didn't know who the mastermind behind it all was. We still had no idea who this Slender Man really was. Would we ever know? Or was it going to remain one of those mysteries that was never solved?

73

NOVEMBER 2014

W e slept in the next morning, since it was Saturday. I enjoyed reading the morning paper that was all about the assassination attempt on Lisa Rasmussen. Suddenly, it seemed that all the sympathy had turned, and now everyone was talking about how heroic Lisa Rasmussen was, and she was compared to big leaders in the world who had also had assassination attempts against them. It was very strange how the mood could turn like this. Furthermore, Jonna Frederiksen had decided to pull out of the race.

""Politic is too dangerous,"" she was quoted as saying. "Life is too short."

"I guess Lisa Rasmussen will end up being our new mayor then," I said to Morten, while sipping my coffee.

He was still smiling after this morning's wonderful sex. My body might be twenty pounds on the heavy side, but I still had it.

"I guess so," he said.

Sophia came over a little later, carrying her son's computer in her arms. "Here, take this," she said. "I don't want it in my house anymore."

I looked at Morten. "I can't have a computer in my house. Not while the investigation is still going on," I said.

Morten shrugged. "It's not the best of ideas."

I looked at the laptop. It was a very nice laptop, and I really missed having a computer. I still had all of my stuff on the card in the hollow chess-piece. I could work on my book and get it finished.

"Maybe I can just keep it somewhere they won't find it."

"Suit yourself, Emma," Morten said. "But I think it's a bad idea."

I grabbed the computer from Sophia's hands, and she left to be with her children. I put it on the table and turned it on.

"You're crazy for doing this," Morten said.

I shushed him and he rolled his eyes before he continued reading his paper. I went to the bathroom, and when I returned, Victor was sitting by the laptop. His fingers were dancing across the keyboard while Brutus was watching from the floor. I watched Victor. It had been awhile since I had last seen him this engaged in something. Could it really be that he was so good with computers? It gave me hope for his future. I knew when Victor was interested in something, he would typically learn everything there was to know about it. Like with his trees and the rocks he gathered. He could end up being quite the computer genius if he wanted to.

A computer genius, huh? Even if he's considered challenged in so many other areas? Who would have known? Hm. What if...

"I wonder," I said to Morten.

"Hm? What's that?"

"We need to go," I said. "I'll tell Maya to look after Vic."

Morten protested. "Now?"

"Yes, now."

A few minutes later, we were in the car. I was driving. I had found Per's home online and set the GPS.

"So, why are we going to this home again?" Morten asked tiredly.

"There's something I need to check," I said.

"The guy is heavily retarded. I really don't want to spend my Saturday looking at some guy drooling on himself."

"Morten, that's not a nice thing to say. You don't have to look if you don't want to," I said, and turned onto the small dirt road leading to the home that was located on what used to be an old farm.

A tall blond nurse greeted us at the door. She gave us a friendly smile.

"Per Larsen? Well, I've never. In all the years I've worked here, no one has ever came to visit him, and now he's had two visitors in one week. I know the first was an officer, but still. Are you friends of the family?"

"We're actually related. His mother was my grandmother's sister. I just heard of his existence recently," I said.

"Well, come in. Per's in his room. He likes his quiet time here before lunch."

74

<hr>

NOVEMBER 2014

The tall nurse knocked carefully on the door to Per Larsen's room, then opened it. "You do realize he can't talk, nor understand what you're telling him?" she asked before she let us in.

"Yes, we understand," I said.

"Alright then. Per? You have visitors."

An old man in a wheelchair looked at us from the corner of the room. With his hands, he pushed the joystick on the electric wheelchair to make it move forward.

"So, he doesn't understand anything at all?" I asked.

Per Larsen stopped the chair. His head was hanging to the side, and he had trouble looking at us. Drool was running down his chin and had wet his clothes.

"To be honest, we don't know how much he understands. He seems to get some of the things we tell him, yet at other times, there's no connection at all. He just got the computer behind him a few months ago, along with all the rest of the residents at the home, and he seems to enjoy playing on it. So I guess he does understand some things. Now I'll leave you alone. Call me if you need anything."

The nurse closed the door, and we were alone with Per Larsen, who was sitting completely still in the chair, looking at us out of the corner of his eye.

Morten exhaled. "Are you happy? You've seen him."

I kneeled in front of Per Larsen and tried to look into his eyes. "Hello Per. My name is Emma Frost. I think you can hear me. I think you can understand and hear me perfectly, can't you?"

Per Larsen didn't react. A couple of moaning sounds escaped his mouth. I glanced around his room, and my eyes fell on the computer in the corner.

"So, you like computers, do you?" I asked.

"Come on, Emma. Let's go home. This is ridiculous."

"I don't think so."

"Emma," Morten said, but I didn't listen. I walked to the computer and pressed the keyboard. The screen turned on. *Minecraft* was open.

"Like to play *Minecraft,* do we?" I asked and pressed login. I heard the wheelchair move behind me. Per Larsen turned, and now I was certain he actually looked at me.

"All this because they hit you with the car?" I asked. I entered the game and didn't have to go any farther. His profile was wearing a skin he had designed himself. Maya used to do the same thing. His character in the game looked exactly like Slender Man, with the black suit and tie and the expressionless face.

Per Larsen approached me from behind. Morten came closer too. "I think you need to call Allan," I said.

"You really think he's Slender Man?" Morten asked.

"I not only think it, I know it. And when the police get this computer and go through it, they'll know it as well. He used those kids to get his revenge. They ruined his life back then."

I kneeled in front of Per Larsen, who groaned loudly. I had a feeling he was trying to speak. Our eyes locked for a second and I felt his sorrow, his deep profound sadness.

Morten called Allan, who came to the home with Officer Tim and I told them everything. They confiscated the computer as part of the investigation. Morten and I decided to leave it all in their hands and drove home. On our way back, I spotted someone riding her bike on the street. I hit the brakes of the car.

"What are you doing?"

"There's still one person who knows what really happened to Per Larsen, and who knows why Per wanted this revenge so badly. See, the way I figure it, everyone thought he was completely lost to the world. It wasn't until he got the computer and tried to use it that he realized he suddenly had a way of communicating with the world for the first time since he'd been hit by the car at only six years old. He came up with the idea of using the kids he got to know through *Minecraft*. He probably read about Slender Man and about the teenagers in the States, and came up with the idea of impersonating this myth that many kids online believe in, the myth of Slender Man. But what makes you want revenge that badly after so many years? Certainly not an accident."

I got out of the car, and as soon as Jonna Frederiksen saw me, she jumped off the bike.

"We need to talk," I said.

EPILOGUE
NOVEMBER 2014

"What about that one over there?"

I pointed at a golden retriever in the corner. I had always wanted a golden retriever, since I thought they were the nicest dogs in the world. But Maya had already set her heart on a small black curly-haired dog that kept barking at everything and everybody and biting his friends at the shelter.

"No, I really want this one," she said.

I sighed. "But it looks just like Kenneth, and it seems to be just as misbehaved. You really think that's a good idea?"

"That's why I like it," Maya said.

I smiled as I watched Maya pick up the small curly-haired dog. It was a crossbreed, they told me. Someone had found it in the street and given it to the shelter, so they had no idea how old it really was or where it came from. It wore no collar.

"Probably left by some German tourists who couldn't take care of it anymore," the red-haired lady named Camilla said.

"I want him," Maya said with stars in her eyes. "I'll call him Kenneth II."

"You're the one responsible for him then," I said. "You have to take care of him and feed him and walk him."

"Of course."

I looked at the red-haired woman. "We've made our choice."

While Camilla finished the paperwork, and Maya held Kenneth II in her hands looking happier than ever, I thought about how much had happened since we had been there last. Luckily, Jonna Frederiksen had told me everything and repeated it to Officer Allan. She had explained how Ulrik Larsen had killed the old man on the farm next to theirs because of what he had done to Peter, and then about how they wanted to beat Per Larsen up to shut him up, but he had run into the street and they had hit him with the car. I got a feeling it felt good for her to finally be able to tell the story and get it off her chest.

Lisa Rasmussen won the election, since she had no opponent, and she promised on the local TV to make sure there would be no lay-offs at the police station, since we needed every one of the officers we had here on the island. She was very grateful for their service, especially since they had saved her life during the assassination attempt. I was very pleased that she would fight for my boyfriend's job.

Morten had gotten his job back. Since he had helped solve the three murders, the chief of police in Esbjerg called him in and told him the charges against him were dropped after they had seen the footage of Dr. Sonnichsen admitting to having framed him with the email, and later by paying someone to beat up Michael. I was also acquitted of my charges, since they couldn't find any evidence against me, since my computer had been destroyed. PE wasn't too happy about dropping the charges, but they had no choice, my lawyer told me. I just had to be more careful in the future, I had to promise her.

The three teenagers were convicted of murder and sentenced to juvenile prison, all three of them obtaining psychiatric help for their problems. Christoffer escaped with nothing worse than the fright.

They had examined Per Larsen's computer and found lots of material, enough to take him to trial, even though it would be hard to put him in a prison worse than the one he was already in. At least he would never be let near a computer again, Morten had told me.

The charges against Dr. Sonnichsen were major, and still piling up, as far as I knew. Morten did most of the investigating, and I knew it was quite extensive. I was certain she was going away for a very long time. Finally, that story was over. She was out of my life, and my family and I could move on. Tonight, I was taking Morten folk dancing downtown.

"All you need to do is sign right here," Camilla said, and pointed at the dotted line. I glanced at Maya right before I put the pen to the paper, then signed my name.

"There you go," Camilla said. "The dog is yours. Good luck."

The End

Want to know what happens next? Get the next novel in the Emma Frost Mystery series here: http://www.ama-zon.com/Where the Wild Roses Grow

AFTERWORD

Dear Reader,

Thank you for purchasing *Needles and Pins*.

I hope you enjoyed it.

The idea for this story actually appeared when I heard that back in the sixties and even seventies, many Danish parents of autistic children were told that they should simply forget about their children while they were put in a home.

The doctors told the parents to pretend the child had died and go have another one.

Many autistic people in Denmark have therefore grown up in homes and never known their families or where they came from.

I later read an article about a man who became autistic after being hit by a car, and that gave me the idea for what happened to Per.

Don't forget to check out my other books if you haven't already read them. Just follow the links below. And don't forget to leave reviews, if you can.

Take care,
  Willow

Tired of too many emails? Text the word: "willowrose" to 31996 to sign up to Willow's VIP text List to get a text alert with news about New Releases, Giveaways, Bargains and Free books from Willow.

ABOUT THE AUTHOR

The Queen of Scream aka Willow Rose is a #1 Amazon Best-selling Author and an Amazon ALL-star Author of more than 80 novels. She writes Mystery, Paranormal, Romance, Suspense, Horror, Supernatural thrillers, and Fantasy.

Willow's books are fast-paced, nail-biting page-turners with twists you won't see coming.

Several of her books have reached the Kindle top 20 of ALL books in the US, UK, and Canada.

She has sold more than six million books all over the world.

Willow lives on Florida's Space Coast with her husband and two daughters. When she is not writing or reading, you will find her surfing and watch the dolphins play in the waves of the Atlantic Ocean.

———

Cover design by Juan Villar Padron,
https://juanjjpadron.wixsite.com/juanpadron

Special thanks to my editor Janell Parque
http://janellparque.blogspot.com/

———

CPSIA information can be obtained
at www.ICGtesting.com
Printed in the USA
BVHW032256200421
605423BV00002B/18